DEADLY DECISIONS

The three of them watched as the Indians dismounted and relieved the three dead men of their valuables. Only after they were done did they all look up at the remaining three riders.

"They're gonna want the woman," Denver said.

"Maybe," Fargo said.

"The only chance we have of gettin' out of this alive," the gunman said, "is to give her to them."

"That's not an option," Fargo said.

"I'm not dyin' for her," Denver said.

"If you try to give her to them," Fargo said, "I'll kill you myself."

"Big deal," Billy Denver said, "what do I care who kills me, you or them? Dead is dead."

Fargo hated to admit it, but he had a point. . . .

THE
TRAILSMAN
#207

CHIMNEY ROCK BURIAL

by

Jon Sharpe

A SIGNET BOOK

SIGNET
Published by the Penguin Group
Penguin Putnam Inc., 375 Hudson Street,
New York, New York 10014, U.S.A.
Penguin Books Ltd, 27 Wrights Lane,
London W8 5TZ, England
Penguin Books Australia Ltd,
Ringwood, Victoria, Australia
Penguin Books Canada Ltd, 10 Alcorn Avenue,
Toronto, Ontario, Canada M4V 3B2
Penguin Books (N.Z.) Ltd, 182–190 Wairau Road,
Auckland 10, New Zealand

Penguin Books Ltd, Registered Offices:
Harmondsworth, Middlesex, England

First published by Signet, an imprint of Dutton NAL,
a member of Penguin Putnam Inc.

First Printing, February, 1999
10 9 8 7 6 5 4 3 2 1

The first chapter of this book originally appeared in *Oregon Outrider*, the two hundred and sixth volume in this series.

 REGISTERED TRADEMARK—MARCA REGISTRADA

Printed in the United States of America

The Trailsman

Beginnings . . . they bend the tree and they mark the man. Skye Fargo was born when he was eighteen. Terror was his midwife, vengeance his first cry. Killing spawned Skye Fargo, ruthless, cold-blooded murder. Out of the acrid smoke of gunpowder still hanging in the air, he rose, cried out a promise never forgotten.

The Trailsman they began to call him all across the West: searcher, scout, hunter, the man who could see where others only looked, his skills for hire but not his soul, the man who lived each day to the fullest, yet trailed each tomorrow. Skye Fargo, the Trailsman, and the seeker who could take the wildness of a land and the wanting of a woman and make them his own.

Nebraska, 1860
Where the shadow of Chimney Rock falls on
the graves of many early settlers
of the West. . . .

1

Skye Fargo's presence in Council Bluffs, Iowa, was unplanned. His intended location had been Omaha, but his Ovaro had picked up a stone bruise on the hoof of his left foreleg. Council Bluffs had been the closest town and Fargo had walked the stallion there.

As it turned out, Council Bluffs not only had a blacksmith, but a vet. The blacksmith removed the horse's shoe and the vet took a look at him. He pronounced the animal fit, but said the leg would need at least a week for the bruise to heal.

That had been five days ago and Fargo was starting to go stir-crazy. Even though he'd met a woman while in town, that only took care of his nights. His days were spent walking around town, or sitting in front of his hotel, going to the saloon when it opened. He'd exchanged more words with the bartender at the Buckhead Saloon than he had with anyone in months.

He was on his way to the Buckhead Saloon when he saw a woman being buffeted back and forth among three laughing men, across the street in an alley. It was the fact that it was happening in an alley that caused him to cross over. Also, the woman was calling for help.

As he got closer he could see that she was an attractive

woman in her early thirties. On the other hand, the men were all in their twenties. He didn't know who had a beef with whom, but three men against one woman made it easy for him to pick sides.

"Please," the woman was saying, "stop . . . someone help . . ."

One of the men had just pushed her toward another when Fargo elbowed him aside roughly, bouncing the man off a wall. As the man slid to the ground, stunned, Fargo approached the other two.

"Okay, fun's over," he announced. "Leave the lady alone."

Fargo was taller and wider than all three of them, but up close it was easy to see that they were drunk.

"Get lost, mister," one of them said. "This ain't your business."

"Please, sir," the woman said, "help me. Get me away from these men."

"Forget it, mister," the second man said. He was holding her by the shoulders. "This is my girlfriend."

"You're a little young for her, aren't you, son?" Fargo asked.

"Well, you're too old for her," the man replied.

"Never mind," Fargo said. "Just let go of her and there won't be any trouble."

"You're the one lookin' for trouble," the first man said. "Why'd you hit my brother like that?"

"Son—" Fargo said, but he stopped when he saw a familiar look in the young man's eyes. "If you go for that gun, friend, I'll have to kill you. Is it worth your life to have a little fun at this lady's expense?"

The man on the ground began to stir and rise. Fargo

took one step and kicked him in the head just hard enough to stun him again.

"Jesus, mister," the second man said, "stop hittin' our brother."

"Let the lady go."

"We didn't mean no harm," the first man said.

"Okay," Fargo said, "no harm done. Let her go, pick up your brother and move on."

The two men exchanged a look, and then the first one nodded and the second one let her go.

"Come on, Richie," they said, helping the other man to his feet.

"What happened?" he asked.

"We'll tell you later," the first man said, and then they walked off, supporting him between them.

"Are you all right, miss?" Fargo asked.

"I think so," she said. "They didn't really hurt me, but I was getting dizzy."

"Why were they doing that to you?"

"I don't really know," she said. "I approached them to ask them for help, but they seemed to prefer . . . pushing me around."

Fargo took a moment at look to her. The way she dressed spoke more of the East than the West. The dress would have looked fine at a tea party with its ruffles and such, but it was out of place on a dusty western street.

She had dark hair that had been pinned up on her head, but tendrils of it had been shaken loose by the treatment she'd received. She was really quite pretty, with blue eyes and pale skin and a very appealing cleft chin.

"You look like you could use a drink," he said.

"Oh, I don't indulge, thank you," she said, "but could

you recommend a place for coffee or tea? You see, I just arrived on the stage."

"Why not go to your hotel?"

"I haven't registered at a hotel yet. Can you point me toward one?"

"Is this the help you were asking them for?" he asked.

"Well, no . . ." In that moment she seemed to take a good look at Fargo for the first time. "Perhaps you can help me, though."

"Well, the nearest hotel is—"

"No," she said, "I mean with my problem."

"Your problem?"

"Yes," she said. "Would you have some time to listen to me?"

"Miss," he said, "it just so happens all I have is time."

The lady introduced herself as Grace Viola. Fargo escorted her to the nearest hotel, where she was able to secure a room. Then they went into the dining room, where she ordered tea, he ordered coffee, and they both ordered some apple pie.

"What brings you to the West, Miss Viola?" he asked.

"It's Mrs.," she said, then added, "I'm a widow."

"Oh, I'm sorry. A recent widow?"

"Fairly recent," she said. "My husband was a minister in Philadelphia. He died some months back."

"And you decided to come out West?"

"Actually," she said, "I don't like the West very much. I didn't like it the first time I was here."

"And when was that?"

"About twelve years ago," she said. "I was a young woman then, newly married. My husband then—not the same man, mind you—decided we should come West. We got this far and joined a wagon train, but no sooner had we started our trip across Nebraska then he fell prey to a snakebite."

"He died?"

"Yes."

Fargo thought that this woman didn't seem to have much luck with husbands.

"Then what happened?"

"Well, I went on with the wagon train but . . . I was pregnant, you see. Eight months along."

"Your husband took you on a trip of that nature while you were that pregnant?"

"I'm afraid so."

"What happened?"

"What you would expect," she said. "I went into labor early, and the child—a boy—did not survive."

Jesus, he thought, if this woman didn't have bad luck she'd have no luck at all.

"What happened then?" This was the most interesting conversation he'd had in days.

"Well, some folks were kind enough to bury the child and then stay behind with me while I recovered. By that time, however, I had decided to return East. The West had taken enough from me."

"How did you get back?"

"Well, the people who stayed with me wouldn't go back, but before long a wagon did appear going the other way. Another family who had suffered a loss also decided to turn back, and they were kind enough to take me with them."

"This is quite a story," he said.

"Yes, I suppose it is," she said. "I returned to Philadelphia and it took me quite a while to recover mentally from my double loss."

"I can imagine," he said. "You're to be commended for recovering at all."

"Well, I did, but it was still quite a long time before I met another man I thought I could love."

"Your minister husband?"

"No," she said, "another man who managed to get himself shot before we could marry. I met my husband—the minister—when he presided over my fiancé's funeral."

Fargo was starting to wonder if all of this was true. How could one person experience all this hardship?

"I see."

"I fell in love with him eventually, and we married. We lived together for six years before he, too, died."

"Violently?"

"No," she said, "he fell ill and simply passed on."

"I'm sorry."

"So you see, I had to make this trip back here."

Fargo frowned.

"Uh, no, I guess I don't see, Mrs. Viola."

"Please," she said, "call me Grace."

"All right, Grace," he said. "Why do you feel you had to come back West? And back here?"

"Well, I have no family back East," she said.

"They died, too?"

"My parents died when I was quite young," she said. "I was raised in an orphanage. In fact, that's where I met my first husband. He and I both grew up there and when we were old enough, we left together and married. You see, no one ever adopted us. When a child gets to a certain

14

age—well, most people want small children, to raise as they see fit."

"I see."

The story—if completely true—got sadder and sadder by the moment.

"Zackary—my first husband—insisted he wanted to come West . . . but I've been through that."

"Yes," Fargo said. "We were talking about why you would come back here."

"Yes, we were."

She put her teacup down and placed her hands in her lap. She stared very solemnly across the table at Fargo.

"Mr. Fargo, my child—my only child—is buried out there. You see, once I lost him I could no longer have children."

Fargo was now surprised that this woman had not taken her own life long ago.

"Now that my husband is gone I want to find my child and give him a proper burial."

"After all these years?"

She nodded.

"It's something I feel I have to do . . . in here," she said, clasping her hands to her breast where her heart was.

"Well, I suppose that's understandable," he said, and he was about to wish her luck when she spoke first.

"Can you help me find that grave?"

It was then he knew he should have minded his own business.

2

Fargo stared across the table at her.

"Excuse me?"

"I was asking if you could help me find my baby."

"Your baby."

"Oh, don't worry," she said, "I'm not crazy. I know the baby is dead. He's been dead many years, but the remains . . . I'd like to find the remains and give them a proper Christian burial."

"Mrs. Viola—"

"Grace," she said, "remember?"

"Grace," Fargo said, "do you even remember where you buried, uh, him."

"Well," she said, "I know we got past Chimney Rock, but not much past it. I could still see it."

Fargo had to admit that narrowed it down, some.

"I'm sorry," she said. "You probably have something important to do."

"Actually," he said, "I've been stuck here waiting for my horse's foot to heal."

"And when will that happen?"

"Well, he should be fine in another two or three days," Fargo said.

"I can wait that long," she said. "I know I'll have to

buy some clothes, and a horse . . . and of course I intend to pay you."

"Grace—"

"I hope you'll do it."

"Grace—"

"But you really don't have to decide now," she said. "Why don't you take some time and think about it?"

"I don't think—"

"Please?"

Her eyes became much bigger and seemed to bore into him.

"All right," he said. "I'll think it over."

She reached across the table to cover his hands with hers.

"Thank you, Mr. Fargo," she said. "That's all I ask."

"Well," he said, patting her hands, "while I'm thinking it over you might as well call me Skye."

"All right, Skye," she said. "Well, I have some shopping to do."

"Maybe you shouldn't walk around town right now," he suggested.

"Why not?"

"Well, those three men might still be around—"

"Oh, I think you've sufficiently scared them away," she said. "I'm sure I'll be fine. First, however, I think I'll go to my room and rest up from my journey."

She stood up and looked at him.

"Why don't we meet in the morning for breakfast?" she suggested.

"Fine," he said, "I'll come to your hotel at nine."

"It really was fortunate for me that you came along," she said.

"Yes," he said, "I guess it was."

Later, while Grace Viola was in her room, there was a knock at the door. When she opened it one of the three men from the alley was there.

"Come in, quickly," she said, "before someone sees you."

Once in the room he said, "You didn't tell me my brother was gonna get kicked in the head."

"I didn't know," she said. "I'm sorry."

"That Trailsman is a tough character," he complained. "I think we should get more money."

"We agreed on an amount, Mr. Lacy," she said.

She went to the dresser in the room, opened the top drawer and took out an envelope. She carried it across the room and handed it to him.

"It's all there," she said. "The amount we agreed on."

"My brother's got a knot on his head, and a bruised shoulder."

"Which made it all look very real," Grace Viola said. "You did what I paid you to do, Mr. Lacy, you and your brothers, and I thank you. Now, please leave."

Lacy opened his mouth as if to protest again, then closed it, shook his head, and left the room.

Fargo took a turn around town to think over Grace Viola's offer. His stopover in Omaha could certainly be put off, there was no great rush for that. And he had been very bored these past five days—except for the nights, of course. And it did seem a rather easy job, not quite the needle in the haystack he had thought it sounded like, at first. His heart certainly went out to the woman for all the hardships she had endured. Maybe finding her baby's remains and burying them properly would help her get a new start.

By the time he returned to his hotel—not the same one Grace was staying in—he had pretty much decided he would help her. He wasn't ready to tell her that, though. He'd sleep on it and talk to her in the morning, if he still felt the same way.

Of course, Amanda McDuff hadn't been letting him get all that much sleep at night, and tonight would probably be no different.

He decided to go over to the saloon for a beer.

"Ed, I have a question for you."

"Go ahead and ask," said Ed, the bartender.

"Three fellas, in their twenties, look enough alike to be brothers. You know them?"

Ed, tall and dark-haired, real slender, rubbed his heavily stubbled jaw.

"Sounds like the Lacy boys."

"Lacy?"

"That's right."

"What do they do?"

"Not much of anything," Ed said. "Sort of the town ne'er-do-wells, you might say."

"Hmmm."

"You have a run in with them?"

"Just a little one."

"Wouldn't think those three would do anything to get themselves in trouble with you, Skye."

"Why's that?"

"They're kind of cowardly, to tell the truth."

"Well, they were doing something cowardly when I met them," Fargo said.

"What was that?"

"They were ganging up on a woman."

"Ganging up on her?"

"Oh, they weren't hurting her, just sort of pushing her around from man to man. I don't know, maybe they were planning to rob her."

Ed rubbed his jaw again.

"Doesn't sound like them," he said. "Ain't never heard of them pickin' on a woman."

"First time for everything, I guess," Fargo said.

"And when you came along I'd figure them to cut and run."

"Well, they didn't run, but they didn't put up a fight, either."

"Still sounds kinda odd to me."

"Well, it's all over now," Fargo said.

"Who was the woman?"

"Somebody from back East," Fargo said. "Wants me to help her find her baby's grave."

"Lots of graves along the old wagon train route," Ed said. "How she gonna know which one is her baby's?"

"I don't know," Fargo said. "Maybe it's marked."

"Lots of those grave markers were just temporary," Ed said. "How long ago we talkin' about?"

"About twelve years."

"Wouldn't think a marker would last that long."

"Maybe she's just got a good memory," Fargo said.

"Well, I wish you luck," Ed Gorman said. "Don't know why anyone would want to find a grave after all these years, though."

"She says she wants to give the child a decent burial," Fargo explained. "Seems she couldn't have any more children after that one."

"That's too bad," the bartender said, "but I don't envy you digging up the remains of no baby."

"Hmmm," Fargo said, "come to think of it, neither do I."

"Hope she's payin' you well," Ed said. "Doesn't sound like your kind of job."

"She's paying," Fargo said, although they hadn't discussed how much. "Don't know who else's job it would be, though. After all, I've just got to find a gravesite by a trail."

"Well," Ed said, "you're gonna find a lot of 'em. Lots of people lost their lives or just flat out died along that wagon route—and most of them was easterners."

Fargo finished his beer, turned and looked around the Buckhorn, which was just starting to get busy. In one corner he saw Billy Denver sitting alone. They locked eyes and the man lifted his mug of beer in greeting, even though they had not exchanged two words since Denver's arrival two days earlier. Denver was about thirty, and Fargo knew that he had a reputation as a gunman. Fargo had no use for men who made their living with a gun.

Ed leaned across the bar so he could speak softly.

"What's with you and Denver?" he asked.

"Can't say I know, Ed," Fargo said. "We haven't spoken, and yet every time I see him he acknowledges me."

"Maybe it's respect?"

"Maybe."

"He ain't got as big a rep as you, Fargo," Ed said. "You think maybe's he thinkin' of tryin' you?"

"Trying what, Ed?" Fargo asked. "I'm not a gunman."

"But he is."

"And I can tell you I'm not thinking of trying him."

"Still, you do have a reputation."

"Not as a gunman."

"That might not matter to him," Ed said. "Maybe you should talk to him?"

"About what? The weather?" Fargo asked. "I like it better this way."

"I know you ain't afraid of him."

"It's got nothing to do with being afraid, Ed," Fargo said. "I just don't go looking for trouble."

"Well," Ed said, "that sounds smart to me."

"I'm going to head out, Ed. You have yourself a good night."

"Girls'll be down in a few minutes," Ed said. "You lookin' for Amanda?"

"No," Fargo said, "I'll be seeing her later. Just tell her I was by, okay?"

"I will. You're not gonna go and drink someplace else, are you?"

"I'm going to check on my horse and then go back to my hotel."

"See you tomorrow, then."

"See you."

Fargo gave Ed a small salute and went out the door.

At the livery he checked the Ovaro and found him standing easier than he had been. He lifted the hoof to look at it, and it seemed almost healed to him. He figured a couple of days for Grace to finish her shopping, and for him to outfit them, and he and the Ovaro should be ready to go.

He hadn't thought about actually digging up the baby until Ed mentioned it. That part certainly wasn't something he was looking forward to, so he could just imagine how she felt about it. What should they bring along, he wondered, to carry the remains in? Just a blanket?

"Looks like he's standing well enough," the blacksmith said, coming up behind him.

Rex Cahill was a big man so Fargo had heard him coming before he spoke.

"Yeah, it looks good," Fargo said, coming out of the stall.

"Gettin' ready to leave?" Cahill asked.

"Couple of days," Fargo said. "You've got a nice town here, Cahill, but I'm not going to be sorry to put it behind me."

"Can't say I blame you," the big man said. "Wouldn't mind leavin' here myself, but I'll be fifty next year. Too old to change."

"Never too old to change," Fargo said.

"For some, maybe," Cahill said, shaking his head mournfully. "Not me, though."

"Well, you've got your business," Fargo said, "and . . . do you have a family?"

"A wife," Cahill said.

"No kids?"

"No," the blacksmith said, "we was never able to have any."

"That's too bad."

"We wanted 'em bad, too," he said. "You know, we could have adopted a long time ago, but we kept hoping.

People kept coming through here on their way West, bringing kids with them. More than once we coulda had one, you know? Some people thought the trip was too rough for kids, and were ready to give 'em up."

"Really, I'd think it was pretty hard to give up your child."

"Not when you had a bunch of 'em," Cahill said. "People comin' through here with five, six, eight, they was always ready to give one up. I often wonder how many of those kids died, and if maybe we coulda saved one by taking it."

"Guess you'll never know," Fargo said.

"Guess not."

Well, he thought, leaving the livery, Grace Viola knew about her child. She knew what happened to it, and he guessed she was entitled to go back and bury it the way she saw fit.

All she needed was a little help. How long could it take?

3

When the knock came on the door later that night it was
a familiar one. Amanda had been knocking now for five
nights, and he knew the sound of it. He hadn't given her
a key, though. For a man with the Trailsman's reputation,
giving out keys to his room was just not a good idea.

He got up from the bed, walked to the door, and
opened it. She came into his arms, all sweet-smelling and
even sweeter-tasting as she pressed her lips to his, slid her
tongue into his mouth. She also pressed her body tightly
to his, and he enjoyed the feel of it. She was a short girl
but her breasts were big and firm, as was her behind. She
was afraid she was going to get fat when she got older,
but right now she was all valleys and curves in the right
places—places Skye Fargo thoroughly enjoyed going.

They tumbled wordlessly to the bed, undressing each
other with ease brought on by four nights of practice.
When he had her naked her skin glowed in the dim light
of the lamp by the bed. Her nipples were hard and as he
sucked them into his mouth she moaned and took hold of
his head, wrapping her hands in his hair.

As he continued to suck and bite her nipples he slid a
hand over her soft belly, into the tangle of hair between
her legs that was just slightly darker than the yellow hair

on her head. He rubbed his palm over her, feeling the tickle of her pubic hair, and then felt the wetness of her as she grew more and more ready. He slid his middle finger along her oozing cleft and you would have thought she'd been struck by lightning.

"Oh God," she cried. She was loud during sex, he'd discovered that the first night. He also discovered that it excited him to hear her. "Mmmm, oh God, your hands are like magic. Oooh, Skye, when you touch me . . . yes, there! Like that! Oooh, it's heaven . . ."

He continued to stroke her, every so often just dipping the tip of his finger into her, teasing her, making her wetter, more sensitive. Every so often her body would just go taut and then waves of pleasure would rush over her, again and again.

"Never," she said, "neverneverever been like this with anyone before . . . oooh, you're making me . . . there I go again . . . Ummmm . . ."

With each wave of pleasure that rippled through her she knew the sense of loss she was going to feel when he went away. Would she ever be touched like this by another man? Would there ever be another man who just *knew* where to touch her?

Now he moved to straddle her, pressed the spongy head of his rigid penis to her wetness and with just the slightest of pushes, entered her. He slid deeply into her, but did it slowly while she raked her nails over his back and keened into his ear. When he was all the way in she wrapped her legs around and he began to move, in and out, in and out, and she matched his tempo and moved with him.

"Oooh, Skye, yes," she said, "yes, I'm . . . I'm float-ing . . . Mmmmm yes, yes, yes . . . ohhh . . ."

He slid his hands beneath her and cupped her solid but-tocks, pulling her to him each time he moved into her again. When they began to move faster and faster the room filled with the sound of their flesh slapping to-gether. As they grew moist there was just the slightest sucking sound as their skin made contact and then pulled apart, so that there was a slap, then suck, then slap, then suck, until it became almost mesmerizing. . . .

Amanda didn't hear it, though. Her eyes were closed and she had given herself up totally to the sensations of it all. She couldn't hear any sounds they were making, didn't even hear herself speaking as she urged him on and on, cried out for him to take her harder and harder, faster . . . the feelings swelled inside of her, just as they did in him. He tried to control himself, wanting to last as long as he could, wanting it to last for her as well as for himself, but eventually it became just unbearable to fight it, almost painful to try and stop it and then he shouted as he ex-ploded inside of her, and she bit down on his shoulder to keep from screaming. . . .

"What is she like, this woman?" Amanda asked, later.

Once they had caught their breath he told her about meeting Grace Viola, and also told her the woman's whole story.

"She's an easterner," he said.

"No, I mean, what is she like?"

"She's . . . controlled . . ." Fargo said. "Mature . . ."

"Old?"

"Older than you, yes."

27

"Well, that's good," she said, snuggling closer, "but I do feel sorry for her. She's been through so much misery and hardship I'm surprised she hasn't—"

She stopped short.

"Hasn't what?"

"It's too terrible to say," she said. "I'm sorry I even thought it."

"Surprised she hasn't committed suicide?"

"Yes," she said, "that's what I was thinking."

"I thought of it well before you did, Amanda," Fargo said. "I can only assume she's an incredibly strong woman. Maybe all these things that have happened to her have just made her stronger."

"They have to," Amanda said, "or drive her mad . . ."

He'd thought about that, too.

"Are you definitely going to help her?"

"Yes."

"Good," she said.

"Why?"

"Well, that means when you leave and you've recovered her . . . uh, the remains . . . that you'll be coming back here."

"There are other towns out around Chimney Rock."

"This is the biggest."

"What about Omaha?"

Amanda made a face.

"You wouldn't want to go to Omaha."

"Why not?"

"Because, silly," she said, "I'm *here* . . ."

They woke together in the morning and, wordlessly, he slid down her body, kissing her all the way, until his face was between her legs, his mouth moving on her. She wriggled and fidgeted beneath him as he used his tongue, and his teeth, and his lips to bring her to the edge, and then over it. . . .

"I don't know what's better," she said. "The nights, or the mornings."

"Both," he said, lying beside her.

She had him in her hand, holding him, stroking him, caressing him until he was as hard as a rock, and then she slid down and took him in her mouth. She marveled at how hard he got, how the skin underneath his penis almost felt like glass as she sucked him, her head bobbing up and down, grunting a bit each time she took him in, fondling his testicles with one hand while she held him at the base of his penis with the other. She was leaning on his thighs and could feel them begin to tremble as the release built up inside of him and then suddenly he was spurting and she was struggling to take him all in. . . .

"The mornings," he said, still later.

"Huh?"

"I think the mornings are better."

"You don't like the nights?"

"I love the nights," he said, "but you said—"

"I said I wonder which were better," she said, "I can't decide. How can you?"

"Well," he said, "I thought, if you pinned me down and *made* me pick—"

"Well, I won't."

"Okay, then."

They lay side by side, she stroking his semierect penis,

and he stroking one of her big breasts, circling the nipple but never actually touching it. . . .

"When will you be leaving?" she asked.

"Not for a couple of days," he said. "She has to shop, and I have to get supplies, and I've got to make dead sure the Ovaro is sound. I'll have to take him for a ride, first."

"The best thing that ever happened to me," she said, "was when that horse of yours stepped on a stone."

"I won't tell him you said that," Fargo said. "Do you want to get some breakfast?"

He asked her that every morning, and she replied in the same way.

"I need to get my beauty sleep," she said, "but you go ahead."

He leaned over and kissed each of her breasts before getting out of the bed and dressing.

"Is she pretty?"

"What?"

She was lying on her back with her hands clasped behind her head. The sheet was over her, but it molded itself to her every curve.

"I said, is she pretty?"

He made a show of thinking the question over before answering it.

"Yes," he said, "she's very pretty."

"Prettier than me?"

He hesitated a moment, strapping on his gun before answering.

"Different," he said, then. "Pretty in a different way."

"What way?"

"A more *mature* way."

"Ah," she said, with satisfaction, "in an *older* way."

"If you prefer to put it that way."

"I do," Amanda said. "I prefer to think that you'll be out on the trail with this *older* woman for a few days and nights, and then you'll come back to me."

He went to the bed, ran his hand over her body through the sheet, then kissed her and said, "Get some sleep. I'll see you later."

"All right," she said.

He left the room, thinking that it was ironic that this was probably the most he and Amanda had talked during one of their nights—and mornings—together, and most of it had been about Grace Viola.

4

When Fargo appeared in the lobby of the hotel where Grace Viola was staying she was there waiting for him.

"Am I late?" he asked.

"No," she said, "I was early. I'm anxious to hear your answer."

"Why don't we go into the dining room, then?" he asked. "We can talk there."

"You mean it's not a simple yes or no answer?"

"I'm afraid not."

"Well," she said, "then at least it's not a no."

They went into the dining room and did not speak again until they were seated.

"I'm inclined to go along with you on this, Grace," he began.

"But . . ."

"There are some conditions."

"Aren't there always?" she asked. "What are they?"

"Well, basically there's just one," he said. "What I say goes."

"And how does this make you different from other men?" she asked. She hurriedly added, "I'm just kidding. Of course if you're going to be leading the way I'm going to do what you say."

"That includes not arguing when I call off the search," he said.

"What?"

"It's been a while since all this happened, Grace," Fargo said. "You may think you remember where the burial site is, but when we get out there you might be totally confused. If I think we're getting nowhere, I'll call off the search."

She compressed her lips and frowned.

"Is this a problem?" he asked.

"It could be," she said. "What if I don't want to call it off."

"We've got to agree now, Grace, that what I say goes," he told her. "There are going to be other dangers out there, as well."

"Like what?"

"Animals," he said, "predators, the four-legged kind and the two-legged kind."

"You mean like those men yesterday?"

"The Lacys are nothing compared to who and what we might meet once we get out there."

"The Lacys?"

"I asked around about those three men," he said. "They're brothers, local products who are known to be troublemakers."

"You handled them quite well."

"That's because they weren't prepared to face a man," Fargo said. "They thought they were just dealing with a woman."

"Look," Grace said, "I'm sure I know where the burial site is."

"Then you have nothing to lose by agreeing to my conditions, do you?"

"No," she said, biting her lip, "I guess not."

"Then you agree?"

She hesitated a moment longer, then said, "All right, I agree. When can we leave?"

"Day after tomorrow."

"Why not tomorrow?"

"I've got to make sure my horse is fit."

"Can't you get another horse?"

He looked at her and said, "This is my horse."

"Oh, all right," she said.

"Besides, don't you still have some shopping to do?" he asked.

"As a matter of fact, I do."

"And so do I, for supplies. I assume you'll be paying the freight?"

"I'm sorry?"

"I'll need money for supplies," Fargo said, "and then there's the question of my fee."

"Oh, of course," Grace said. "I'll pay you whatever you think is fair, Fargo. As for supplies, I can give you some money right now."

She took a wad of bills out of her purse and counted some out for him.

"Do you always carry that much money?" he asked, accepting the money for the supplies.

"Not always," she said, putting the rest of the money away. "Just for this trip."

"I suggest you put most of it in the bank," he said. "There's no point in taking it all with you."

She studied him for a moment and then said, "That's a

good idea. I'll open a bank account today. Is there anything else I should know?"

"No, but there are things you should have."

"Like what?"

"Well, to start, a horse. Can you ride?"

"Of course."

"Well?"

"Very well."

"Not, uh, sidesaddle."

She smiled and said, "No. I mean, I have ridden sidesaddle, but I can ride in a conventional fashion."

"Then we'll need to buy you a horse, and a saddle. We can get together later today to do that—that is, if you want my help."

"Definitely," she said. "You'll know what kind of horse to choose for the kind of terrain we're going into. I bow to your superior knowledge, here, Fargo."

"Fine. On your own you can buy some trousers and shirts, and a pair of good boots."

"All right. Anything else?"

"Just leave everything girlie and frilly behind, Grace. There won't be anyplace for it where we're going."

"Oh, I know that. Twelve years ago I started out wearing dresses and soon learned the error of my ways, Fargo. I know how to dress for this."

"That's good," he said. "Then I don't have any more suggestions. I'll pick up the supplies we need, and decide if we need a packhorse or not to carry it."

"Will we need that much?"

"Probably not. There will probably be some towns, or at least some trading posts, along the way where we can

35

restock. I'll check with some people here in town and see what they can tell me."

"When should we meet to go and buy the horse and saddle?" she asked.

"How much time will you need to shop?"

"A few hours."

"I suggest we meet here in the lobby of your hotel at three. That gives both of us plenty of time to do what we have to do."

"All right."

They paid their bill and left the dining room. They walked through the lobby and out the front door together, and there they parted company.

"See you at three," she said, before starting off down the street.

That had gone easier than he'd thought. He had gotten it into his mind that Grace Viola was going to be the stubborn kind. Of course, just because she agreed to his conditions did not mean she was actually going to abide by them if and when the time came.

That remained to be seen.

Fargo went to the general store to arrange for supplies that would be picked up the morning they were to leave. He'd decided that a packhorse would not be necessary. They could get by on coffee, bacon, beef jerky, and some canned goods, and could even run cold camps to cut down on the amount of utensils that had to be carried.

He had a conversation with the general store owner about towns between Council Bluffs and Chimney Rock, and was assured that he'd be able to restock without much difficulty.

"You do have some outlaws out there," the man warned, "white ones as well as red ones."

"I'll be on the lookout."

"Do you need any extra weapons?"

He hadn't thought of that. He was going to have to ask Grace if she could ride *and* shoot.

"I don't know yet."

"If you do I can help you here," the owner said. "I've got a good selection of rifles and handguns."

"I'll be back if I need one," Fargo promised. "Thanks."

As he left the general store he almost ran into the sheriff, a man he had been careful to meet only once since he came to town.

"Sheriff Resnick," he said.

"Fargo," Resnick said. He was a sad-looking man with unkempt hair that hung shaggily from beneath his hat. He had bags under his eyes like a man who slept badly, and the belly of a man who ate well.

"You know, when you came to town five days ago I was anticipating trouble."

"Were you?"

"Yes."

"Sorry to disappoint you."

"Well, that's just it," Resnick said, "I was pretty pleased—"

"Glad to hear it."

"Until today."

"What happened today?"

"I got a visit from Les Lacy."

"About what?"

"Seemed you roughed up his brother Wayne. Is that true?"

"Damned if I know," Fargo said. "I don't know one Lacy brother from the other. I had a dustup with three men who were abusing a lone woman. Was that them?"

"Abusing a woman?" Resnick asked.

"She had just gotten off the stage and made the mistake of asking these three men for help," Fargo said. "They helped themselves and started having some fun. Who knows how far it would have gone if I hadn't stepped in when I did."

"Where's this woman now?"

"She's staying in town," Fargo said. "I can bring her over to see you, if you really think it's necessary."

"No, that's okay," Resnick said. "That sounds like something the Lacys would pull, starting trouble and then blaming somebody else. I just had to check on it. You understand."

"Sure, Sheriff," Fargo said, "I understand."

"Will you be staying in town much longer?"

"I'm going to take my horse out for a test ride," Fargo said. "If he's as fit as he looked, I should be leaving day after tomorrow."

"Good," Resnick said, then, "I mean—"

"I know what you mean, Sheriff," Fargo said. "The sooner I leave the sooner you can stop worrying about trouble."

"No offense meant," the sheriff said, hurriedly.

"None taken, Sheriff," Fargo assured him, "none taken."

5

Since Fargo finished with his shopping chores early he decided to go to the livery to see what kind of horses were available for sale. Once he picked a few out he could bring Grace over to see if she had a preference. Watching her check over some horses would give him some idea of how comfortable she'd be around them. Perhaps she rode back East, but someone else always saddled the horse first, and took care of it afterward.

"That Ovaro is in pretty good shape," the liveryman said. "Why are you interested in another horse?"

"It's not for me, it's for a lady," Fargo said.

"Ah . . . well, I've got some nice gentle ponies I could show you—"

"I can't use something gentle," Fargo said. "I need something that will be able to keep up with my horse, and handle any kind of terrain."

"Jesus, Mr. Fargo," the man said, "I ain't got nothing that kin measure up to that Ovaro of yours."

"It doesn't have to measure up," Fargo said, "just keep up for a while."

"Well," the man said, rubbing his jaw, "I do have a couple of seasoned horses out back."

"Let's go and see them."

Together they went out back and Fargo checked over the horses. He found two he liked and picked out three others that wouldn't do.

"When I come here with the lady later this afternoon," he said, "you show us all five."

"I get it," the man said. "Yer testin' her knowledge of horseflesh."

"That's exactly right," Fargo said.

"I gotcha," the man said. "I'll take care of it for ya."

"And haggle on the price," Fargo said, "but don't overcharge, understand?"

"Yes sir, whatever you say. The price'll be fair, you can be sure of that."

"I know I can," Fargo said, giving the man a long look. "I'm counting on you."

"Yes sir!" the man said, this time with more feeling.

When Fargo met Grace Viola in the lobby of her hotel she was wearing some of her new purchases. The jeans she was wearing were brand spanking new, and stiff as a board. The boots also needed some breaking in.

"How do I look?" she asked.

"Real nice," Fargo said, "but we'll have to dirty you up some."

"Excuse me?"

"We'll have to take the crease out of those pants and the stiffness out of those boots before you get on a horse, Grace."

"How do we do that?"

"Like I said, dirt."

"I have to get them dirty?"

"You give them to me later," Fargo said, "and I'll drag them behind my horse some and then give them back."

"But . . . they're brand-new."

"Trust me, Grace," Fargo said, "they may not look as good when I'm through with them, but they'll be a lot more comfortable."

"Oh, all right."

"Now let's go and get you a horse."

"When we buy one," she asked, "are you going to drag it behind your horse, too?"

When they got to the livery the liveryman was all set. He listened to what they "wanted" and then invited them out back to take a look.

"These are the best I've got," he said, indicating the five horses in the corral.

Grace looked at Fargo.

"Are you going to pick?"

"Why don't you?" he asked. "You're the one who has to ride it."

She studied him for a moment, then smiled and said, "All right." She looked at the liveryman. "Before I go into the corral, though, separate the bay and the roan. Those are the only two I'm interested in."

"Why?" the man asked.

"The other three are buzzard bait," she said, and then looked at Fargo. "Am I passing, so far?"

"With flying colors," he said. The bay and the roan were the ones he had picked out, too.

Grace studied the two horses for a while, even felt their legs, checked their conformation, and looked at their teeth. As far as Fargo was concerned there was not much to choose between the two. Either one would have done

41

as well, but now she was trying to impress him, so he just stood back and watched.

"Looks like she knows her stuff," the liveryman said to him.

"I guess so."

"All right," she announced, "I'll take the roan. What's the price?"

The liveryman looked at Fargo, then walked over to where Grace was standing and named a price. Grace scoffed, made a counteroffer, and they haggled like that for a few moments before the liveryman gave in, reacting as if he was being taken advantage of.

"How about a saddle?" she asked.

"I've got some saddles inside," the man said, "but I ain't got no fancy sidesaddles or nothin'."

"Just a western saddle will do," Grace said.

"I got plenty of those."

"Show me a used one," she said, "so Mr. Fargo doesn't have to drag it behind his horse first."

"I got some broke-in saddles," the man said, and led the way back into the livery.

By the time they left the livery Grace had a horse and saddle. The liveryman agreed to have both their horses saddled and waiting for them in two mornings.

"Did I do okay?" she asked.

"You did fine."

"Do I have to pass any more tests?"

"Maybe just one."

"And what would that be?"

"Can you shoot?"

She hesitated, then said, "I *can,* but not well. I'm not going to be able to pass any marksman tests."

"You don't need to," he said. "All I want you to be able to do is point and fire."

"I can do that."

"Then let's go over to the general store and pick something out for you."

"Rifle or handgun?" the man asked.

Fargo looked at Grace.

"I've fired both, but I don't think I want to wear a holster on this trip."

"A rifle will do."

"Got a right nice Henry I took when a feller couldn't pay his bill," the man said. "I can make you a good price for it."

"Talk to her," Fargo said. "It's going to be her gun."

"Oh, I see."

Again Fargo stood back while Grace ironed out the price of the Henry with the general store owner, and when they left she had the Henry and a box of shells with her.

"I guess I'm ready," she said, "unless there's something else?"

"No, nothing else," Fargo said. "Once we get on the trail you can show me how you shoot, but for now I think we're done."

"Then maybe we can leave tomorrow?"

"No," Fargo said, "I haven't taken my horse out, yet, to see how his foot is."

"When do you figure to do that?"

"Well, I thought I'd do it after I saw you back to your hotel."

"Why don't I go out with you?" she suggested. "You can see me ride, and I can get the feel of my new horse."

"Well, all right," Fargo said. "Let's go back to your hotel anyway to leave your rifle in your room. You won't be needing it."

"That's fine with me," she said. "I'm actually looking forward to doing some riding."

"How long's it been since you last rode?"

"I have to admit it's been a while," she said, "but after we've gone a few miles I should be settled into the saddle."

And after a few hundred miles, he thought, she was going to be complaining of a pretty sore butt—a pretty butt, but a sore one.

6

While Fargo saddled the Ovaro he watched Grace saddle the roan. She had very little trouble tossing the saddle up on the animal, and then cinching it in tight. It was obvious, at least, that she had saddled a horse before.

When she finished, she turned, leaned against the horse, and asked, "How did I do?"

"Well, it was okay."

"Okay?"

"You'll have to learn to do it faster," he said. "There might be times on the trail when speed is important, but you'll still have to make sure it's done right."

"Boy," she said, "I can see right now that you're going to be a tough taskmaster."

"Well," he said, "now let's see you ride."

They mounted up and rode out of town. Fargo kept the pace easy on purpose, since she had already admitted that it had been a while since she was in the saddle. When she was able to keep up with him, though, he quickened the pace, and varied the terrain.

While watching her, he also kept a wary eye on the Ovaro for the slightest sign that he might be favoring that hoof, or keeping weight off the leg.

"How is he?" she asked, after a while.

"He's moving well," Fargo said, "and doesn't seem to be favoring it at all."

"Does that mean we can leave in the morning?"

"Absolutely."

"I guess you've probably made some friends in town that you want to say good-bye to."

"No one in particular," he said. "Just some acquaintances."

"Surely there must be a girl?"

"Oh," he said, "yes, of course there's a girl. How did you know?"

"A man like you," she said, "I'm sure you always have women around you. I'm sure they, uh, like you very much."

"And I like them very much. See that hill?"

"Yes."

"Let's go up it at a fast pace."

"Is this a test for me," she asked, "or for your horse?"

"For both," he said, and fed his heels to the Ovaro.

He got to the top of the hill well ahead of her. The Ovaro had taken it flawlessly, and each stride had put space between himself and the roan.

To her credit, when Grace saw that she couldn't keep up she decided not to punish her mount. She took the hill surely, not abusing the animal, and was smiling when she got to the top.

"You didn't actually expect me to keep up, did you?" she asked.

"No, I didn't."

"I didn't think so."

"It's enough that you made it."

"So I passed?"

"Yes," Fargo said, "you passed."

"And my horse?"

"He passed, too."

"And your horse?"

"Oh yes," he said, "him, too—"

"Good—"

"—with flying colors."

She frowned.

"Now let's get back to town and rub them down," he said. This was the part he was really interested in now. To see if she knew how to take care of a horse after she'd ridden it.

"Do you want to race back?" she asked.

"No," he said, "let's take it at a nice, easy pace."

"Good."

He wasn't sure, but he thought she might have been favoring her butt a little.

Back at the livery they unsaddled the horses, rubbed them down, and fed them, and she did quite well there, too.

"I'll bet," she said, when they were done, "you thought I always had someone else do this part for me."

"The thought had crossed my mind."

"Well, have we put your mind to rest about me and horses?"

"Yes," he said. "You know your way around them—"

"Thank you."

"—well enough," he ended.

She shook her head and said, "Yes, sir, a tough taskmaster."

He walked her back to her hotel and said, "Take it easy the rest of the evening and I'll come by in the morning to get you."

"What time?"

"Eight a.m."

She winced, but said, "Fine. I think I'll soak in a hot tub."

"A little sore?"

"No," she said, but he knew she was lying, "I just don't know when I'll get another chance."

"Make sure you bring your Henry," Fargo said. "I'll have the supplies ready and, if I'm early enough, I'll have the horses saddled and out front."

"All right," she said. "I guess I'll see you in the morning."

"See you then."

She turned and went into the hotel. She seemed to be aware that he was watching, and she was trying to walk normally, in spite of the fact that her butt had to be pretty sore.

It was then that he remembered he still had her jeans, and had to get the stiffness out of them. He'd have to take care of that and bring them around to her later so she could put them on in the morning.

Fargo entered his hotel room sometime later and threw Grace's broken-in jeans onto a chair. He moved about the room and packed whatever belongings he had into his saddlebags. Within moments, he was packed to leave

Council Bluffs—and not a moment too soon. Except for Amanda, his stay here had been boring—other than his little set-to with the Lacy brothers, and his meeting with Grace Viola. At last he'd be doing something worthwhile, like reuniting a mother with her child—her child's *remains*. And he'd also be getting paid for it.

The sun was still out, and with nothing left to do in his room he picked up the jeans and left. Walking through the lobby holding the jeans he felt foolish, as if he'd been hired to do Grace's laundry.

Mentally, his fee for finding her dead baby's grave went up.

At Grace's hotel he decided to simply leave the jeans at the desk to be brought up to her.

"Any message, sir?" the clerk asked.

"No," Fargo said, "no message."

"Who shall I say they're from?"

"She'll know who they're from."

The clerk looked at them as they lay on his desk, dusty and abused.

"They're dirty."

"I know that," Fargo said. "They're supposed to be."

"Why?"

"Could you just have them brought to her room, please?" Fargo snapped. He'd had enough of talking about Grace Viola's jeans. He decided to go and let the sheriff know that he'd be leaving town in the morning.

That was something that would make the two of them happy.

*   *   *

"Will you be coming back?" the sheriff asked when he heard the news.

"I doubt it," Fargo said. "When we find what we're looking for I think I'll just keep moving on."

"Well," Resnick said, "for the sake of the lady I hope you find it."

"I hope so, too."

"It won't be easy," the lawman said, "but I guess if anyone can, you can. I mean, that's what you do, right?"

"Right," Fargo said, "I find babies' graves."

Which, at least, would be better than staying in Council Bluffs any longer.

The next one he had to tell about leaving was Amanda. He went to the Buckhead Saloon, but she wasn't yet working the floor. In the same corner he saw Billy Denver sitting, nursing a beer. Just for a moment Ed's suggestion about talking to Denver echoed in his head, but he disregarded it. He didn't know what he'd have to talk about with a grown man who still went by the name of Billy.

"Beer," he said to the bartender, Ed.

"Amanda should be down in a few minutes," Ed said, setting the beer in front of him. "You leavin' town?"

"How did you know?" Fargo said, picking up the beer.

"You got that look."

"What look?"

Ed frowned and said, "The look of a man who's leavin' town."

"I didn't know there was a specific look for that," Fargo said.

"There is when you're in my job," Ed said. "There's a look for almost everything."

"Well, I guess you have to have been a bartender for a long time to recognize them."

"Sure do," Ed said, leaning on the bar. "I couldn't teach that to somebody, you know."

"I'm sure you couldn't."

He wasn't leaving town a moment too soon. These were the kind of conversations he'd been having with Ed all week, and *they* were the *interesting* ones.

"I'm going to sit in a corner and wait for Amanda," Fargo said.

"Nobody'll come over and talk to you, you know," Ed said. "They're all intimidated by you—except me."

Fargo smiled a humorless smile and said, "I know."

7

Amanda took the news well because it was no surprise. It was simply a confirmation of what they had talked about the night before.

"At least we'll have one more night together," she said, then asked, "We will, won't we? I mean, you don't have to spend it with her, do you?"

"No," he said, "I'm going to spend it with you."

She looked relieved and said, "I have to go to work, so I'll see you later."

As she went about her work he finished his beer and prepared to stand up and leave when the batwing doors opened and the three Lacy brothers came in. One of them had a bandage around his head, which was visible from beneath his hat.

Fargo sat back down.

These three interested him. According to the bartender, Ed, what they were doing to Grace Viola was unusual. Apparently, the sheriff didn't feel the same way. He just felt they were troublemakers, in general. Since Fargo had spoken with both men he felt qualified to say that he put more credence in Ed's opinion than in the lawman's.

He watched the three brothers walk to the bar and order beers. He noticed that Ed kept looking his way, expecting trouble. Fargo didn't have trouble on his mind. He had no beef with the brothers, but they might have one with him. If they did, though, that was their problem, and he decided to go ahead and stand up and leave, as he had intended.

To get to the door he had to pass the bar, and in passing the bar he had to pass them. As he did so Les Lacy, the oldest, saw him and nudged his brother Paul. The third brother, Stan, was the one with the bandaged head.

"Your name Fargo?" Les called out.

Fargo stopped and turned his head to look at them.

"That's right."

"We didn't mean no harm, Mr. Fargo," Les Lacy said, with more respect than Fargo would have expected. "There weren't no call for you to go and kick my brother the way you did."

"From what I saw," Fargo said, "a lady needed help. There were three of you, and one of me, so I had to make a point. I'm sorry your brother was the one I had to make it on."

"If you'd just told us who you was," Les Lacy said, "we woulda stopped what we was doin' and been on our way."

"I'll remember that for the next time," Fargo said.

"Ain't gonna be no next time," Lacy said, "no sir. We don't aim to tangle with you again. Fact is, we'd like to buy you a drink and bury the hatchet."

"I don't have time for a drink," Fargo said, "but consider the hatchet buried. You and I have no beef with each other, boys."

"That's mighty kind of you, Mr. Fargo," Les Lacy said. "Mighty kind."

Fargo left, totally confused by the Lacy brothers. He hadn't expected them to be so respectful the next time they met. They were no great danger to him, but he didn't like when people seemed to go against type. It usually made him think they had something up their sleeves.

He wondered what they had up their sleeves.

"What was that all about?" Stan Lacy asked his brother. "All that 'Mr. Fargo' stuff. That feller kicked me in the head, Les, and I wanna—"

"Relax, Stan," Paul Lacy said. "Les knows what he's doin'."

"Well, I don't know what he's doin'."

"When that lady paid us did you see the money she had in her purse?" Les Lacy asked.

"I saw it," Paul said.

"I didn't," Stan said.

"Well," Les said, "it was there, and a lot of it—and she's probably got more in the bank, back East."

"What good does it do us back East?" Stan asked.

"It don't do us no good," Les said, "but we can make her get it."

"I'm for that," Paul said, rubbing his hands together.

"And then there's that other thing she told us about," Les said.

"What other thing?" Paul asked.

"You mean that dead baby stuff she was talkin' about?" Stan asked.

"You believed that?" Les asked.

"Whataya mean?" Stan asked.

"She's got somethin' buried out there, all right," Les said, "but I don't believe it's no dead baby."

"Whataya think it is, Les?" Paul asked.

"I don't know," Les said, "but we're gonna find out."

"How?" Stan asked. "We ain't no match for that Trailsman feller."

"But you would like to get him back for what he done, right?"

"Damn right," Stan said.

"Well then," Les said, "all we need to do is find us a little help."

"How we gonna do that?" Stan asked.

"We're gonna look, brother," Les said, smiling, "we're just gonna look."

Fargo went back to his hotel to have dinner alone in the dining room. After that he went to his room to wait for Amanda. Time was dragging. He wanted it to be morning so he and Grace could be on their way. When the knock came at his door it was not Amanda's knock, but a different one. It was also too early to be her. He went to the door with his gun in his hand and opened it.

"Do you really need that?" Grace asked, looking at the gun.

"Not now that I know it's you," he said. "What can I do for you, Grace?"

"Can I come in, or do I have to stand out in the hall?" she asked.

"Come on in," he said, backing away.

He put the gun back in the holster, which was hanging on the bedpost, then turned to face her. She was wearing another dress that would have been fine in the East but was out of place in the West. He could also smell that she'd had her bath. What he couldn't figure out was what she wanted. He also didn't want her to be there when Amanda arrived.

"I won't stay long," she said. "I'm sure you have . . . plans for the evening . . . and the night."

"Is something wrong?"

"I was just . . . thinking," she said, "sitting in my room alone, thinking. Thank you for the trousers, by the way."

"You're welcome. I hope they'll feel all right when you put them on."

"I'm sure they will."

"What were you thinking about?"

She looked down, then back up.

"Unfortunately," she said, "I was thinking about my baby."

"Oh."

Fargo didn't know what to say to that, or how to react, so he just remained quiet.

"Oh, don't worry," she said, "I'm not going to turn into a weepy female. I did all my crying for Edward a long time ago."

"Edward?"

"Oh, that was the baby's name," she said. "I didn't tell you that?"

"No, you didn't."

"Yes, when he was born—I mean, stillborn—and I realized he was a boy, I named him. You see, that's another reason I want to . . . bury him properly. I was such a mess back then that the other people I was with buried him, and without a marker."

"I see. If he had a name, he deserves a marker."

"Exactly," she said, "you *do* understand."

"Yes."

"Even if that marker has the same date of birth and date of . . . death."

"I do understand."

"I'd better go and get some sleep now," she said. "I need a walk, and found myself near your hotel. I guess I just came up to say good night—and thank you."

She moved to him to kiss his cheek but abruptly she turned her head and kissed his mouth. It went on for longer than a simple good night kiss, and he thought suddenly of Amanda. Grace smelled good, and he could feel the heat coming from her body, and if Amanda wasn't expected . . .

"I'm sorry," she said. "That wasn't . . . I'm just sorry."

"No reason to be sorry, Grace," he said. "I should walk you to your room."

"No, no," she said. "I'll be fine. I'll see you in the morning . . . Skye."

"Good night, Grace."

After she left he went to the window and watched her walk down the street until she was out of sight. After that he went and sat on the bed and wondered what the nights on the trail were going to be like.

The next knock on his door was the more familiar one, and it came a couple of hours later. Amanda came into his arms as soon as he opened the door, kissed him, then backed away, sniffing.

"She was here," she said.

"Who?"

"The woman," she said, "the woman with the dead baby."

"Grace?"

57

"If that's her name."

"How do you know she was here?"

"I can smell her," Amanda said, removing her wrap. She was still wearing her work dress, which was very low-cut. "She came here straight from a bath, too."

"Amanda—"

"Did she try to get you into bed?"

"No—"

"Did you go to bed?"

"No—"

"I'll be able to smell her on the sheets if you did, you know—"

He took her by the shoulders to keep her from doing so and held her in place.

"You have an amazing sense of smell," he said. "Yes, she was here. She was taking a walk and stopped in to say good night."

"That's all?"

"I told you this night was for us," he said. "I haven't lied to you yet."

"No," she said, "you haven't. I'm sorry."

"It's all right."

She sat down on the edge of the bed and started removing her stockings. Fargo stood back and watched her with pleasure.

"She just wanted to say good night?"

"Well, she also told me the name of her dead baby."

"What was it?"

"Edward."

"It lived long enough to be named?"

"No," he said. "It was stillborn, but when she saw it

58

was a boy she named him. However, he was still buried without a marker."

"Oh no . . . so that's why she wants to find him, then? To give him a marker?"

"I suppose so."

She stood up and removed her dress, then pulled him to her.

"I hope you find him, Skye."

"I do, too."

"But I don't want to think or talk about her and her baby anymore tonight—and I don't want you to, either. Promise?"

"I promise."

She was naked, her hands were on him, and it was a very easy promise to make. . . .

8

They crossed the Missouri River into Nebraska and traveled a half a day before they had to stop for the first time for Grace. Since it was her expedition Fargo didn't utter a word of complaint.

"I'm sorry," she said, "I guess it's been longer than I thought since I've been on a horse."

"That's okay," he said. "We'll rest awhile until you feel like going on."

She sighed and went to sit on a rock, then hissed and stood up.

"Just sit slower," he said. "I'll take care of the horses."

While he was doing that she lowered herself gingerly onto the flat rock until she was finally seated. When he returned he was carrying her Henry.

"What's that for?" she asked.

"I thought while we were resting you could show me how well you can shoot."

"I didn't say I could shoot well."

"You didn't say that you shot badly, either," he said. "I just want to see which one you're closest to."

"Do we have to do it now?" she asked. "I just sat down."

He also had a canteen with him so he sat next to her,

set the rifle down, and passed her the canteen. She took a few sips of water and passed it back to him.

"This is going to take longer than we thought, isn't it?" she asked.

"Probably not."

"It will if we have to keep stopping for me."

"Well, we'll just have to do with you what we did with your pants."

"Drag me behind your horse?"

He smiled and said, "We just have to get the creases out, break you in a bit, that's all. The pants fit really well, don't they?"

"Yes," she said, dubiously, "but I don't like comparing myself to a pair of pants."

"Let's just say that after a few days you won't be so sore."

"I was sore after that first ride we took," she complained. "Now I'm worse, instead of better."

"Take my word for it," he said. "It won't last. Come on, show me how you can shoot."

He handed her the Henry and she stood up with it.

"What do you want me to shoot at?"

"That tree," he said. "It's about as wide as a man. Put one right in the center."

She lifted the rifle, fitted the stock to her shoulder, aimed, and fired. She took a chip off the edge of the tree as the bullet glanced off.

"I hit it."

"If that was a man he'd still be coming at you," Fargo said, standing up. "Lift the rifle again."

She did, same as she had before.

"Now, before you fire, get comfortable. Make sure it

61

fits right against your shoulder, press your cheek to it . . . that's it . . . now when you fire don't jerk the trigger, just squeeze it."

She did as he said and fired again. She missed the center of the tree, but the bullet thudded solidly into it instead of glancing off.

"That would be a rib," she said.

"Which still wouldn't guarantee that he'd stop coming at you. We'll work on it."

"Who's going to come at me, Skye?" she asked. "I don't understand."

"You never know what's going to happen out here, Grace," Fargo said. "It pays to be careful. Let's try again."

They worked a half hour and by that time she was hitting the tree square in the center.

"That's good," he said. "Very good. You're a quick learner."

"Can we stop now?" she asked.

"Sure," he said. "We can work on firing quicker another time."

"Fine," she said, dropping her hands as if the rifle were weighing them down.

"Are you ready to ride again?"

"Oh sure," she said, "my shoulder is so sore I won't even notice my butt anymore."

"Reload the rifle and then we'll be on our way," he said.

He went to get the horses while she reloaded, and then they mounted up. She slid the rifle into the scabbard on her saddle.

"Eventually," he said, "you'll learn how to shoot from horseback."

"When I hired you I didn't realize it included being a gun instructor."

"You should learn to shoot," he said, "even if it's just for hunting purposes."

"Speaking of which," she said as they started off, "do you have all our supplies in that sack?"

She indicated the burlap sack that was hanging from his saddle.

"It's all there," he said.

"What's all there?" she asked. "It doesn't look like much."

"The essentials are there," he said. "Anything else we need we can pick up along the way."

"If I remember correctly," she said, "it took days, weeks before we reached Chimney Rock."

"I'm sure you do remember correctly," he said, "but remember you were traveling by slow-moving wagon, not on horseback. We can cover three times the distance, this way."

"If my butt holds up," she muttered.

He laughed and said, "I think your butt will hold up just fine."

They camped that first night and he made coffee and handed her some beef jerky.

"This is all we have to eat?" she complained. "No hot food?"

"Grace," he said, "to carry enough supplies to make this trip comfortable we would have needed a packhorse, and a packhorse would have slowed us down. I assumed you were in a hurry."

"Well . . . not exactly a hurry. I mean, there's no time limit. I just thought—you know, some hot food would be nice."

"We'll have hot food in the morning," he said. "It'll be more important then. It's better to travel on a full stomach than sleep on it."

"I suppose."

"Remember," he said, "I'm in charge."

"Oh, I remember," she said, tearing off a piece of jerky with her teeth.

After they ate he told her to unroll her blanket and get some sleep.

"What are you going to do?" she asked.

"Just sit up for a while," he said. "I was in Council Bluffs too long. I missed being on the trail."

She tried to lie down, rolled around a few times, then looked at him.

"You missed sleeping on the ground?"

He smiled.

"You get used to it after a while. Just lay your head on your arms. Believe me, your body is tired. You'll fall asleep."

"I doubt it," she said, but in minutes she was breathing deeply and evenly.

Fargo stayed awake longer than he'd intended. There was really no reason to be on watch. He wasn't trailing anyone, and no one was trailing him. Still, he felt uneasy about going to sleep. He watched Grace sleep for a while, watched the stars in the sky. He walked over and checked on the horses, added some wood to the fire to keep it going, made another pot of coffee.

When he finally went to sleep he slept fitfully. He kept waking and looking over at her. The only thing he could figure was that someone was following them, and he could *feel* them. Maybe the Lacys had decided to get some revenge. Or maybe they had seen how much money Grace carried. He'd meant to ask her if she'd opened the bank account and left most of the money behind. He'd have to do that in the morning.

The next time he awoke it was starting to get light. Again he saw to the fire, made some coffee, and then he fried up some bacon. The smell of the food woke Grace, who sat up and rubbed her face.

"You were right," she said. "I did sleep."

"I know," he said. "I watched you for a while."

She dropped her hands into her lap and looked at him. "Why?"

He shrugged.

"Nothing better to do, I guess."

He handed her a cup of coffee, which she accepted with a "Thank you."

"Bacon should be ready soon," he said.

"Good," she replied, "I'm starved. Did you sleep? Or did you just watch me?"

"I slept some," he said. "Did you open a bank account, like we talked about?"

She sipped her coffee before answering.

"I totally forgot."

"So you've got your money with you?"

"Yes," she said. "Why? Do you want to get paid now?"

"No," he said. "I just have this feeling . . ."

"About what?"

"That someone may be following us."

"And you think they're after my money?"

"Could be."

"Who knows I have it?"

"Maybe the Lacys."

"They're afraid of you."

"Maybe," he said.

He put some of the bacon into a plate and handed it to her, then made a plate for himself.

"Let's eat and get moving," he said. "I might be able to tell something then."

"Maybe you were right," she said.

"About what?"

"About me learning to shoot more accurately," she said. "It might come in handy, after all."

9

"Can you make anything out?" Grace asked.

Fargo was standing in his stirrups, looking behind them. It had been three days now since he felt they were being followed, but he still hadn't been able to make anything out for sure.

"No, nothing."

"Maybe you're wrong," she said, sounding hopeful.

"I hope I am."

He sat back down in his saddle and looked at her.

"You look like you're sitting on your horse a lot better today."

She smiled.

"It's amazing. I guess I've managed to build up callouses on my butt. I'm actually starting to enjoy the ride."

"How about sleeping on the ground?"

She stretched her back and said, "I haven't gotten the hang of that yet, I'm afraid."

"There's a town a few miles ahead," he said. "We can restock there."

"How can you tell that?"

"I can just about see it."

"That far?"

"It's all flat."

"Are we close, yet?"

"To Chimney Rock?" he asked.

"Yes."

"No," he said. "We've got another week ahead of us—less if we push the horses, but I don't want to do that—not to yours, or mine."

"All right," she said. "You know best."

"Let's keep moving."

They rode in silence for a while, and then she asked, "This worries you, doesn't it?"

"What does?"

"That there may be someone following us and you can't see them?"

He took a deep breath and then looked at her.

"Yes, it worries me. This is supposed to be what I do. If there is someone on our trail I should be able to spot them."

"What are some of the reasons why you might not be able to?"

"There are a few," Fargo said. "If it's one man and he knows what he's doing he'd be hard to spot. If it's more than one—say four or five—they could be riding far apart, so that their dust clouds don't mingle and form one big one."

Her eyes widened.

"I never thought of that," she said. "That's so . . . smart."

"Thank you," he said, "but I didn't invent it. There are ways to read sign and track, and there are ways to read your back trail. Right now, though, none of them are working—and yes, that worries me."

*　　*　　*

They rode in silence again, and Grace was alone with her thoughts. Had she made a mistake in hiring those Lacy brothers? She'd only wanted them to help her attract Fargo's attention, but maybe—instead—she had attracted theirs. Fargo might be right about the money. She probably should have left it in the bank, but she thought she might need it along the way.

If Fargo was right and they were being followed then it had to be the Lacys and someone else. They would be too afraid to face Fargo, just the three of them.

She touched her rifle, glad now that Fargo had been tutoring her in the firing of it. Of course, having to use a rifle to shoot a man wasn't something she had bargained for.

In the end, though, it would all be worth it.

The town was a very small one called Scottsville. As they rode down the main street, though, they could smell the fresh lumber and see the new buildings going up, so it was growing. Fargo was glad of that. The first thing a growing town did was make sure it had a good general store.

And a saloon.

"Are we going to stay long enough for a bath?" she asked.

"It's up to you," he said. "I hadn't thought about spending the night, but like we said before, we're not in any great hurry."

"I know I sound like a baby," she said, "but a bath would really feel nice."

"We can check into the hotel for one night," he said.

"That might give whoever is following us a chance to catch up, and then maybe we can get a look at them."

"Do you think it's those men? The Lacy brothers?" she asked.

"Don't know who else it could be."

They took the horses to the livery, where a cheerful liveryman told them what a great town this would be to settle down in and raise kids. Grace smiled, and Fargo ignored the comment.

They walked to the hotel—the only one in town—and approached the front desk.

"Hello, folks," the desk clerk said, as cheerful as the liveryman had been. In fact, he could have been the liveryman. Fargo wondered if the man would have had time to run over and come in a back door.

"How about a nice room with a view of the street?" he asked.

"How about two?" Fargo said.

"Oh, sorry," he said, "thought you were married. Sure, we've got two rooms." He turned and got two keys while Fargo signed them both in. "Here you go. Need some help with luggage?"

"No luggage," Fargo said, "just these." He hefted his saddlebags.

"Well, enjoy your stay and let us know if we can do anything for you while you're here."

"The lady would like a bath."

"Sure thing. I'll have it drawn up and waiting for you, ma'am, in just a few minutes."

As they turned to walk away from the desk Grace asked, "You're not going to take one?"

"Oh—uh, sure, after you, though," Fargo said. "And after I go and take care of getting the supplies."

"Oh."

They went up the stairs to their rooms and stowed their saddlebags. Fargo also had the burlap sack, which was almost empty now.

"I'll check in with the local sheriff," he said, "while you take a bath."

"Why would you do that?"

"I'd like to get to know him before he comes looking for me—or us."

"Why would he?"

"Because we're strangers," he said, "and that's his job."

"Will you tell him you think someone is following us?" she asked.

"No," Fargo said, "we're just passing through. He wouldn't care about that. Come on, I'll walk back down with you."

She got a fresh shirt from her saddlebags and wished she also had a fresh pair of trousers. She realized that people who traveled on horseback for days at a time wore the same clothes, but she wasn't used to it.

Down in the lobby Fargo said, "I'll knock on your door in a little while and we'll get something to eat."

"I just thought of something," she said, clutching at his arm.

"What?"

"What if you don't?"

"What if I don't what?"

"Knock on my door," she said. "What if you walk out that door onto the street and you don't come back?"

71

"Why would I do that, Grace?"

"I'm not saying you would do it on purpose," she said. "What if something happened to you?"

"Nothing will."

"I'd be stuck here."

"Grace—"

"It would be like last time—"

"Grace," he said, shaking her a little. The lobby was empty so no one was staring at them, except for the desk clerk.

"Why are you starting to panic?" he asked. "You have to relax."

"I know, I know," she said. "It's just that—oh, I don't know what it is. I'll be all right."

"Are you sure?"

"Yes, yes," she said, "go on."

"You sure you don't want me to hold your hand while you take a bath?"

She giggled and said, "That would give the desk clerk something to talk about, wouldn't it?"

"I guess so."

She released her hold on his arm and said, "You go ahead. I'll wait in the room for you."

"Okay," he said. "Just relax and enjoy your bath, all right?"

"Sure."

"Go on, now."

She walked to the desk and the clerk took her back to where the tubs were. Fargo turned and left the hotel.

10

Once Fargo was outside the hotel he changed his mind. He decided to grab a chair and sit for a while, watching the street to see if anyone rode in. If there was someone following him that he couldn't see, he'd like to meet the man. Of course, even if they did ride in it probably wouldn't be for hours.

He decided to give it a couple of hours and then get something to eat with Grace. Seeing the sheriff could wait, but he underestimated the initiative of the local law. While he was sitting there a man crossed the street and approached him, and he could see the sun glinting off his very shiny badge. He'd seen lawmen like this before, men who spent time polishing their badges. Most of them spent more time on that tin star than they did taking care of their guns, but he couldn't make that judgment about this man.

Not yet.

" 'afternoon," the sheriff greeted him.

" 'afternoon, Sheriff."

"My name's Shepherd," the man said, "Sheriff Tom Shepherd. Just get into town?"

"Actually," Fargo said, "we got here a couple of hours ago."

The sheriff was young, probably not yet thirty-five—maybe not even thirty-two, kind of young for a town sheriff. Usually, a man that age was still working as a deputy.

"Actually," the sheriff said, "a little more than that. You've been sittin' here for at least that long."

"Have I?"

"Yes sir," the lawman said, "you have. The question is why?"

Fargo looked up and down the street and it was then he noticed that he could see the bank from where he was.

"Why would you be watching this street for so long when you just got to town?" the lawman asked.

"I was just waiting," Fargo said.

"Waiting for what?"

"To see if any friends would ride in after me."

"You expectin' some friends?"

Fargo realized he'd taken the wrong tact. The sheriff thought he was waiting for his gang to arrive so they could rob the bank.

"I think we're getting off on the wrong foot, Sheriff," he said.

"Why don't you tell me what the right foot would be?" Shepherd asked.

Before Fargo could answer Grace came walking out of the front door, and she was wearing one of her dresses. Fargo didn't even know she had brought one with her. This one was kind of distracting, because it was tight enough to show off her full bosom, and also showed her arms.

"I thought you were going to take me for something to

eat?" she said to Fargo. She looked at the sheriff then. "Hello."

"Ma'am," the sheriff said, removing his hat. "You know this fella?"

"Well, of course I know him," she said. "We rode into town together. I don't know you, though."

"I'm sorry, ma'am," the lawman said, "I'm Sheriff Tom Shepherd."

"Sheriff Shepherd?" she asked, smiling. She looked at Fargo. "I bet you can't say that three times in a row, very fast!"

"I don't know if I'd want to try," Fargo said.

"Sheriff, my name is Grace Viola. My friend here is Skye Fargo."

The sheriff looked at Fargo very quickly.

"The Trailsman?"

Fargo just looked at the man.

"I'm sorry," he said, "when I saw you sittin' here for so long I thought—well—"

"Thought what?" Grace asked.

"He thought I was watching the bank," Fargo said.

"Really?" she asked the sheriff. "Is that what you thought?"

"Well, yes, ma'am," Shepherd said. "I did. You see, that's my job, to think like that."

"Well, I'll bet you do your job very well, Sheriff . . . and your badge is so shiny."

"Well . . . I try to give a good appearance."

"And you succeed. If you don't mind, though, Mr. Fargo did promise to feed me." She looked at Fargo. "I guess I took too long and the sheriff got suspicious because you were waiting for me. I'm sorry."

"That's all right," Fargo said, standing up. "Maybe the sheriff can tell us a good place in town to get something to eat."

"Sure can," Shepherd said. "There's a little café just about a block away, this side of the street. It's called Emma's. Best steaks in town."

"Much obliged, Sheriff," Fargo said. "We'll give it a try."

"Yes," Grace said, "thank you very much."

"My pleasure, ma'am."

Fargo and Grace began walking down the block. Fargo didn't turn but he could feel the sheriff's eyes following them.

"That was very good," he said to Grace.

"I remembered what you said about the sheriff finding you," she said. "The clerk told me you were sitting out here, and then I saw out the window that the sheriff was crossing the street. I put two and two together."

"Your arithmetic is very good."

"I thought you said you were going to go to him before he could come to you?"

"I decided just to watch the street, first."

"To see if anyone else would ride in?"

He nodded.

"Did you see anyone?"

"No."

"Then maybe you were wrong."

"Maybe."

They walked a little further and then Grace said, "Here we are."

The name EMMA was painted into the big plate glass window. They went inside, were seated by a middle-aged waitress, and both ordered steaks. From their table they could see out the window.

"We can still watch from here," Grace observed.

Fargo nodded.

"If we don't see anyone by the time we leave," she went on, "isn't there some way to lose them?"

"We could try," he said, staring out the window. "We'd have to push the horses harder than I'd like to."

"Maybe we should try that."

He looked at her.

"It's hard to lose someone when you're not even sure they're there."

"How do we make sure?"

"Well," he said, "I could double back, but that would mean leaving you alone."

"Oh." She obviously didn't like that.

"That wouldn't really work, though."

"Why not?"

"Well, eventually they'd reach the point where I doubled back," he said. "If they can read sign they'd know I did it. That would tip them off that we know they're following us."

"If there is someone following us."

"Right."

"Which we don't know."

"Right."

"And we probably never will."

"Unless," Fargo said, "they make a move."

"Like trying to kill us?"

"Or rob us."

"Maybe," she said, "I should go to the bank in this town and put some of the money in it."

"Too late for that, if they already know about it," Fargo said.

"But that way if they do rob us they wouldn't get it all."

"Grace," Fargo said, "if they rob us, they'd kill us, too."

"Oh."

The waitress came with their steaks then and they started to eat.

"I'm glad you came with me," Grace said. "I mean, alone I wouldn't know any of this stuff you've been telling me. If the Lacys had taken the job they probably would have killed me and robbed me by now—or worse."

"It's all right," Fargo said. "I'm not going to let anything happen to you."

"I just want to find my baby," she said. "Maybe if we told them that—"

"Men like that wouldn't care about that, Grace," he said. "You can't talk to them, especially since I already embarrassed them once."

"Would they kill you just for embarrassing them?" she asked.

"Oh, yes," he said. "Men have killed for a lot less—but let's not forget your money. Put the two together and they'd kill us for sure."

She shuddered and said, "The world can be a pretty scary place, sometimes."

"I know it."

* * *

They finished eating and still did not see anyone ride into town.

"They could be waiting outside of town for us to start moving again," Fargo said.

She put her hands to her temples and said, "There are just too many possibilities to think about. Why can't they just let me find my baby?"

"Let's not forget another possibility," he said.

"What's that?"

"That I'm wrong."

"Somehow," she said, "I don't think that's a possibility. Why did the sheriff call you the Trailsman?"

"It's a reputation I have."

"You mean like . . . a legend or something?"

"Not a legend," he said, "just a reputation. It's also what I do. People just have to come up with names for other people. It's like a game they play—particularly if they're newspaper people."

They paid their bill and left the café.

"Well, the sheriff was right about that," Fargo said, outside. "The food was pretty good."

"Yes, it was. What do we do now?"

"Well," Fargo said, "if I remember correctly, you asked me to take a bath."

"I didn't mean—"

"It's all right," he said, smiling. "Believe me, I take baths, sometimes."

11

Fargo was in the bathtub, enjoying the way the hot water was soaking into his skin. His gun was on a chair next to the tub, within easy reach. He'd had baths interrupted before by gunfire, and he had learned his lesson the first time.

When he heard the door open he reached for his gun, but arrested the move when he saw that it was Grace.

"I'm sorry to barge in," she said, looking sheepish.

"What is it?"

She closed the door and stood with her back against it.

"I hate to admit it," she said, "but I guess I'm scared. I mean, we don't know if someone is following us, and I'm sitting up in my room alone just waiting for someone to kick the door in."

"Do you want to stay here while I finish up, Grace?" he asked.

"Well, I don't want to rush you. I'll stay if you just continue doing what you're doing."

"Okay," he said. He wasn't embarrassed to have a woman in the room while he bathed. He'd been with enough women in his life for modesty not to be a problem. Unfortunately, he could smell her from where he was—that fresh, clean scent that only women seem to get when they're fresh from a bathtub—and he was reacting to it. If he leaned back and tried to relax in the tub he knew his erection would just pop up out of the water.

"Have you done your back?" she asked.

"What?"

"Your back," she said, and suddenly she was behind him. "I could wash your back for you."

There was a sponge nearby, which he hadn't been using, and she picked it up, reached over his shoulder to dip it in the water, and he knew that she could see how hard he was. He was relaxed about it now, though, because at least now he knew what was going to happen.

He leaned forward and she began to scrub his back with the sponge. She reached into the water again to wet it and when she did he realized that she had taken off her shirt. Her full breasts pressed into his back, her hard nipples poking him. Suddenly, her mouth was on his neck and the sponge was floating in the water, ignored. She moved around to the side of the tub so he could see her. She was naked to the waist, but she bent now and peeled her trousers down her legs, and kicked them away. She knelt by the tub, reached into the water and took hold of him. He crouched down so that his penis broke the surface of the water. She kept him in her hand, stroking him with her thumb.

"Get in," he said, "get in with me."

Her eyes shining, she lifted one leg over the rim of the tub, then the other, and slid in across from him. He felt her legs on either side of him. She sat forward, took his penis in her hand again, and reached down with the other hand to fondle his balls.

He reached for her, slid his hands over her wet, glistening breasts, which were full, with heavy undersides and large nipples. He reached further then, so that he was able to grip her by the waist and pull her to him. She bent her knees as she came to him and he lifted her up and set her down on him. As he pierced her she gasped and put her head back, her eyes closing.

"Oh God," she said, "I knew it would be good . . . but this is almost too good . . . Ooooh, Skye, yes, yes, oh, yes . . ."

He slid his hand beneath her slippery buttocks and began to lift her up and let her down so that she was riding him. She put her arms around his neck and arched her back, and he leaned forward to kiss her breasts and bite her nipples.

"Are you still frightened?" he asked her gently.

"Shut up," she said. "Shut up and fuck me."

She kept riding him that way, leaning forward to bite or be bitten, kiss or be kissed, until he swelled inside her and then erupted, sending water sloshing over the edge of the tub as she writhed on him. . . .

They dried off and dressed quickly and hurried up to his room. Once inside they discarded their clothing again and fell onto the bed in a hot embrace.

He slid down her body this time and pressed his mouth to her.

"Oooh, God, Skye, your tongue . . . oh, oh, ohhhh . . ."

His tongue moved over her, tasting her, teasing her, entering her, finding her, flicking her, circling her, bringing her to the edge and then drawing back . . . and starting again.

"You're . . . gonna . . . kill me . . . that way . . ." She gasped, her hips twitching, her butt bouncing up and down on the mattress.

He kept his mouth there until she made a noise in her throat and went tense, biting her lip to keep from screaming. . . .

He was on her then, and in her, before she had a chance to recover.

"Ooooh," she growled, wrapping her legs around him, pulling him to her, biting him, scratching him, imploring him never to stop. . . .

"Harder, Skye, oh yes, harder, please . . . come on, come on!"

He slammed into her harder and harder as she begged him to, commanded him to, as she lunged up at him every time he drove into her and then she tensed again for the explosion that was to come. As she bucked again he felt his own release gush from him. It felt as if she were *sucking* him, taking more and more from him when he thought he had no more to give, and the pleasure became almost painful as she squeezed him inside of her saying, "More, more . . . more!"

"I guess we've wasted money on two rooms," she said later, with her head on his shoulder.

"You're paying the bills," he reminded her, and she slapped him on the side. "You go downstairs and tell the man we decided to use one bed."

"I suppose we should have talked about this," she

said. "We both knew it was going to happen, after I kissed you that night."

"Did we?"

"I would have stayed with you then, if you had asked me to . . . but you had other plans."

"Now, now . . ."

"I'm not even going to ask who it was," she said. "The poor girl is still back in Council Bluffs, and I have you now . . . I have you . . ."

As if to prove her point she slid her hand down over his belly and took hold of his penis again. She began to stroke him and he began to swell in her hand. . . .

"Well, we found a way to pass the time," she said, lying on her back with her hands up over her head.

"Yeah, we did that," he said, lying next to her. He reached up to touch his gun, as if to assure himself it was still there.

"You keep that thing close all the time, don't you?" she asked.

"Yes."

"I knew that when you answered the door that night with it in your hand. You're a careful man."

"It's the only way to stay alive."

"I picked the right man for the job, then," she said. "I know you'll keep us alive to find my baby."

"Well, I was your second choice, you remember."

"The Lacys?" she asked. "I didn't know any better. I was just off the stage, looking for help. Anyway, it's thanks to them that we met, so I can't really complain much, can I?"

She sat up, drew her knees up, and wrapped her arms

around them. He ran his hand down the elegant line of her back.

"You women," he said.

"What about us?"

"You're beautiful," he said. "Your shoulders are beautiful, your back, this line that goes down to your butt . . ."

"Are we talking about me?" she asked, with her eyes closed. "Or are we talking about women in general."

"Well, women in general are beautiful creatures," he said, "but some are more beautiful than others. Take you, for instance."

"What about me?"

"You have one of the loveliest backs I've ever seen."

"Do I?"

"Definitely."

She put her head down on her knees as his hand kept rubbing her back.

"Tell me more about me."

"Your breasts."

"What about them?"

"They're nice and round underneath. I like to hold them in my hand and feel their weight."

As he said that he sat up and reached around to do just that.

"And your nipples," he said, touching each of them with his thumb, "are big and beautiful, and a lovely rosy color . . ."

"Mmmm," she said as his thumbs rubbed her nipples. "I have ugly feet."

"What?"

She lifted her head.

"Before you get to my feet and ruin all of this with an obvious lie, I wanted to tell you that I know I have ugly feet."

"What's ugly about them?"

"They're too damned big, for one thing."

"Nothing wrong with big feet."

"I can see what a dangerous man you are," she said.

"In what way?"

"You seem to know exactly how to talk to a woman."

"I also know when to stop talking."

Then he pulled her into his arms, cradled her, and kissed her, a long, wet, searching kiss that went on for a long time . . . and then led to other things. . . .

"You men," she said later.

"Me," he asked, "or men in general."

He was lying on his stomach, the bedclothes long since on the floor, so that he was naked and exposed. She ran her hand over his back, down to his butt.

"I'm talking about you," she said. "You have a lovely butt for a man, so smooth and strong." She ran her hand over his ass, a finger down the crease between his cheeks.

"You know," he said, "I don't think a woman has ever told me that."

"What about your other parts?" she asked. "I'm sure women have told you what a beautiful man you are."

"Hmmm," he said, "I tend to forget the things women tell me when we're in bed. After all, they tend to tell me what they think I want to hear, don't they?"

She slapped his right cheek, a resounding slap that left the red imprint of her hand.

"Ow! What's that for?"

"For making fun of women," she said. "Most men do just what you said to us."

"I know," Fargo said, "but I'm saying that women do it, too."

"You want me to admit that?"

"You don't have to."

"Oh," she said, "you've done enough research on the subject, huh?"

"Lots of research."

She leaned over and gently bit his ass.

"What are you doing?" he asked.

"Research of my own," she said, and slipped her hand down between him and the mattress. . . .

The next time Grace woke up she saw Fargo standing at the window, naked. She kept silent and just watched him. He was standing with his hands at his sides, his legs apart. She could see his testicles hanging heavily between his legs, studied the conformation of his buttocks, his back, his broad shoulders. He looked like a statue someone had cut out of stone.

"What is it?" she asked, finally letting him know she was awake.

"I was wondering when you'd speak."

"You knew I was awake?"

"Yes."

"How?"

"Your breathing."

"And you just let me lie here and stare at you?"

He turned and looked at her over his shoulder.

"It would have given me pleasure to lie there and stare at you."

She shook her head and tossed back the covers.

"You're a remarkable man. You must be cold. Come back to bed and I'll warm you."

He didn't hesitate.

12

They got up the next morning and had breakfast at the same café where they'd had dinner the day before. The food was just as good.

After that they went to the general store to pick up their supplies. They had not risen very early, because they'd had a full night of activity with each other, not to mention the morning. After all, they really weren't in a hurry.

After getting supplies they left the general store and walked to the livery to pick up their horses. They ran into the sheriff along the way. He removed his hat in deference to Grace.

"Leaving town already?" he asked.

"We have to continue our journey, Sheriff," Grace said. "You have a very nice little town here, though."

"I hope to keep it that way, too," he said, "and we hope it won't always be little."

"Well, good luck to you, Sheriff," Fargo said.

"Uh, Mr. Fargo."

"Yeah?"

"As far as I know," the sheriff said, "there were no other strangers in town yesterday but the two of you . . . if that's any help to you."

"Actually, Sheriff," Fargo said, "it is. Thank you very much."

"Sure." The sheriff put his hat back on. "Have a pleasant ride, miss."

"Thank you, Sheriff."

They continued on to the livery.

"Why do you suppose he said that?" she asked Fargo. "I mean, about other strangers?"

"I guess he was taken with you," Fargo said.

"Or impressed with you," she said.

"It doesn't much matter which," he said. "It's useful information. If we do have a tail they decided not to follow us into town."

"What does that mean?"

"It means it is the Lacys."

"How so?"

"It would have to be someone we'd know, or they could have come into town without being worried about getting recognized."

"The Lacys are the only ones that qualify," she said.

"Right."

"Where would they wait for us?"

"Well," Fargo said, "we rode in from the east, so they'd be waiting someplace west of town, where they could see us leave."

"What can we do about that?"

"Well," he said as they reached the livery, "we could go north or south and throw them off our trail. That would add a day to our trip, though."

"What's the difference," she asked, "if we have to travel seven more days, or eight?"

"It's your call," Fargo said. "It's your trip."

"Let's do it," she said. "You pick the direction."

"North."

"How far north should we go?"

"Not so far that we leave Nebraska, but far enough to throw them off. Then we can come at Chimney Rock from the north and still get where we're going."

"And that will throw them off?"

"Well," Fargo said, "it will depend how long they wait when they don't see us coming. And it will depend on how good a tracker they have with them."

They entered the livery and Fargo settled up with the liveryman and told him they'd saddle their own horses. When that was done they both mounted up and rode out of the livery.

"This really is a nice little town," she said.

"There are lots of nice little towns, Grace," Fargo said. "All of them are pretty much the same."

"I guess you've seen a lot of them, traveling the way you do."

"An awful lot."

"Ever find one you wanted to settle down in?"

"Never found the right town and the right woman for that," Fargo said.

"You still might."

He nodded and said, "Anything can happen. Come on, we'll cut through the center of town and then head north."

"I hope this works," she said.

"So do I."

They put some distance between them and the town, moving north, and then stopped.

"Do you see anything?" she asked.

"No," Fargo said, "but the question should be, do I feel anything?"

"And do you?"

He looked at her.

"No."

"How can you be sure?"

"I can't be," he said. "It was an instinct that told me we were being followed, and it's an instinct that tells me that we're not, now."

"And if they find us?"

He shrugged.

"Let's keep moving north until the end of the day," he said. "Tomorrow we'll head west again."

"All right," she said. "You and your instinct are the boss."

They camped that night just before dusk. Grace offered to build the fire and make the coffee and that left Fargo free to care for the horses.

"Unless you think the fire will give us away," she added.

"I don't think that's a problem," he said. "Our tactic either worked or it didn't. If it did they won't see the fire. If it didn't . . ." He shrugged and went off to take care of the horses.

When he reached the fire she had the coffee ready and handed him a cup.

"How is it?" she asked. "I'm not a very good cook."

"As trail coffee goes," he said, "it's pretty good."

"Can we cook something?" she asked.

"Some beans," he said. "That's about it. Let's save the bacon for breakfast."

"All right. Shall I—"

"You made the coffee," he said, "I'll take care of the beans."

He hoped she wouldn't ask him again about her coffee. It was barely palatable, which was why he wanted to make the beans—although how she could have ruined the beans he didn't know . . . but he didn't want to take a chance.

Once the beans were ready, he doled them out equally and handed her a plate.

"Thank you."

They ate in silence, staring at the sky, alone with their thoughts for a while.

"Last night was kind of amazing," she said, finally.

"Yes, it was."

"I suppose . . ."

"You suppose what?"

"I suppose we shouldn't talk about . . . feelings, or anything like that."

"Grace—"

"No," she said, holding up her hand. "Let's forget I said that, okay? I was just being silly."

"You're not silly," he said. "I just don't want us to make too much of this. Last night was wonderful, and I hope there'll be more nights, but I don't think it will lead to anything . . ."

"Permanent?"

"You will be going back East, right? After this is over?"

"Of course," she said. "That's where I live."

"And I live out here," he said. "Eating beans, and sleeping on the ground."

"See?" she said. "I told you I was just being silly. I know all that."

When they finished eating he took her plate from her.

"Get some sleep," he said.

"What are you going to do?"

"I'll stand watch for a while."

"Not all night?"

"No," he said, "I'm just being careful."

"So they don't sneak into camp?"

"So no one sneaks into camp," he said, "them or anyone else who may be out here. Or anything else."

"What do you mean," she asked, "thing?"

"You know," he said, "an animal, a varmint."

"What kind of animals are out here?"

"Lots of things," he said. "Well, you know about snakes."

Of course she did, since her young husband had died of a snakebite twelve years ago.

"There are also cougars, jackrabbits, lizards, all kinds of things."

"Thanks," she said, "I needed to think about that as I go to sleep on the ground."

"Well, generally speaking they steer clear of people," Fargo said.

"That snake didn't steer clear of my husband."

"How did that happen?" Fargo asked as she wrapped her blanket around her. "Where was he bitten?"

She hesitated, then said, "It's kind of embarrassing."

"Not for him," he said. "He's dead."

"You have a point," she agreed, but she still paused before answering. "He was bitten on the ass."

"Ah," Fargo said, "he went and found a place to relieve himself, and squatted on a snake."

"Yes, exactly."

"Well, Grace," he said, "if you squat on a snake, you're going to get bit. We'll just have to make sure we don't do that. Okay?"

"I'm all for that."

"Go to sleep, then," he said. "We'll get an early start in the morning. If we move along briskly we might not lose an entire day."

She lay down, but her eyes didn't close.

"I dream about him sometimes."

"Who?" he asked. "Your husband?"

She shook her head.

"The baby," she said. "My son. Edward."

"Oh."

"In my dreams sometimes he's a baby, but sometimes he's growing up. I've seen him when he's three, I've seen him when I sent him off to school. God, I've even dreamt about him getting married. Isn't that crazy?"

"I don't think so," Fargo said. "If you keep him alive in your dreams he's bound to grow up there."

"You don't think I'm crazy?"

"Not at all."

"Then maybe I'll go to sleep now and dream about him," she said.

"Close your eyes," he said. "Sleep comes faster that way."

"Smart aleck," she said, but she closed her eyes and drifted off to sleep.

13

When Grace woke the next morning it was to the smell of bacon and coffee.

"Did you sleep?" she asked him, accusingly.

"I did," he said, truthfully. "I fell asleep not long after you did and only woke up a little while ago."

She rolled out of her blanket, stood up, and stretched, working the kinks out.

"I don't think I'll ever get used to sleeping on the ground."

"You don't have to," he said. "I doubt you'll be doing it much once this is over."

"You're right about that," she said. "I'm really going to appreciate beds after this little trip."

She came over to the fire and he handed her a cup of coffee and a plate of bacon.

"Thank you."

He sat down to eat his own breakfast and they talked awhile before starting out for the day.

"Tell me, what you're going to do after this is over, Grace?" he asked. "After you give your child a proper burial."

"I'm not sure, Skye," she said. "I know I'll be going back East. I didn't like the West when I was here twelve years ago, and I don't like it now. I don't think I could ever live here."

"But will you go back to Philadelphia?" he asked. "There are lots of other cities in the East."

"I know," she said. "I've been thinking about that, about Boston, or New York. I . . . to tell the truth, I haven't spent a lot of years on my own."

"I don't see why you'd have to," he said. "There are a lot of men who like taking care of beautiful women."

"I'm not sure I want to be taken care of, anymore," she said. "I think I would like to try living on my own, for a while."

"Then that's what you should do."

"I have to admit it scares me, though."

"Well, it should," he said, "since you've never done it before, but I think you can do it."

"You do?"

"Don't forget it took a lot of guts for you to come from Philadelphia to Council Bluffs on your own, Grace," he said.

She thought a moment and then said, "I suppose it did."

"There's no suppose about it," he argued. "Also, it took courage for you to approach three strangers, looking for help. Unfortunately, you picked three men who didn't know how to treat a lady."

"I know," she said, shaking her head, "that was a terrible lack of judgment on my part—but it turned out right. It led me to you—or you to me. If not for you I might be dead . . . or worse."

"Well," he said, "let's not have any more talk about being dead. Come on, we'll clean up and get under way."

*   *   *

Fargo took them north for another hour and then they changed direction, heading east again.

"We were traveling northeast anyway to get to Chimney Rock," he said, "so we really won't be that far off the mark."

"You don't have to convince me," she said. "I'm in your hands."

"Since you're paying me," he said, "I'm just keeping you informed."

She smiled and said, "Okay, Mr. Fargo, keep me informed."

"What do you know or remember about Chimney Rock?" he asked.

"Not much. I remember we could see it from far off. It was a lot bigger than I thought it would be. Some of the people said it looked like a shot tower from far off."

"It does," Fargo said.

"Have you seen it?"

"Once," he said. "I came at it from the other direction, though, not this way. I know it's made up mostly of hard-packed clay and some rock."

"Well," she said, "I *was* going to ask how we'd know when to start south again, but we'll be able to see it, won't we?"

"That's for sure," he said. "I haven't taken us that far north. We'll see it. That'll be our landmark to head south again."

She turned and took a long look behind them.

"Do you think we really lost them?" she asked.

"I think we lost them," he said, "but I don't know for how long."

"What do we do if they catch us?"

"Well, first off," he said, "they can't just catch us. I mean, they won't get that close without us knowing they're coming."

"And second?"

"Once we know they're coming for sure we can take action."

"What kind of action?"

"Well, either evasive—which is what we've been doing—or offensive."

"By offensive you mean . . . we would shoot them?" she asked.

"We could, yeah."

"That means . . . I'd have to actually . . . shoot somebody?"

"Only in an extreme emergency, Grace," he said, "like to save our lives."

She didn't comment on that.

"Do you think you could do that?"

She hesitated, then said, "I don't know."

"Let me ask you this," he said. "The other night in that alley, if you thought those three men were going to kill you, could you have killed them first?"

She looked at him, a sort of bewildered look on her face.

"You know," she said, "it never occurred to me at that exact moment that they might kill me."

"Then why'd you call for help?"

"I thought I needed help to get away from them."

"Did you think they might want to rape you?"

"Well . . . yes . . ."

"And that wouldn't have been enough for you to kill them?"

"I'm . . . afraid I don't think in terms of killing someone, Skye. I—I'm sorry."

"Don't be sorry for being civilized, Grace," Fargo said, "but you sure are proving that you do belong back East, and not out here."

"You're a civilized man."

"But I will kill to save my life," he said, "or to save the life of others. I've done it and will do it with no second thought."

Just for a moment Grace shivered, and then the moment passed. She was counting on this man not only to guide her, but to protect her, as well. She certainly didn't expect him to do that without hurting anyone, did she?

"Grace?"

She looked at him.

"I'm fine," she said. "This just takes some getting used to, that's all. And I guess I'm just realizing that I was in more danger than I thought, that night. I guess I owe you even more than I thought I did."

"You don't owe me a thing," he said. "Just remember you're paying me to do this, all right?"

"All right, Skye," she said, "I'll remember."

As much as he talked about being paid—and she had every intention of paying him—she knew that there were lots more reasons than money for what he was doing.

Lots more.

"There it is," she said, days later. "I see it." She pointed, excited as a child.

"I see it, too."

"So we head south now?"

He nodded.

"Now we head south."

They turned their horses and headed directly for Chimney Rock.

They were a good twenty-five miles from Chimney Rock, and were able to travel all day long in sight of it. They had to cross the North Platte River to get to it, and beyond it.

The rock had a large conelike base, a hundred and fifty feet or so in diameter, which made up two-thirds of its height. From there up the chimney narrowed, growing smaller and smaller toward the top. In total, it was about two hundred and fifty feet high.

"When we get there, Grace," Fargo said, when they were still about three miles from it, "where would the burial site be?"

"Well, it's past the rock," she said, thinking back. "Chimney Rock was on our right and we went on for a few miles. Once we go that far I should be able to find it."

Fargo hoped so. He didn't want to think they had come all this way for nothing, that she wasn't going to be able to find the burial site. Of course, that thought had come into his head more times than he cared to count. What if she couldn't find it? Then what? Would she give up, pay him, and go back East?

"What are you thinking?" she asked.

"I was just thinking—"

"—that I might not be able to find it. Right?"

"How did you know?"

"I can see it on your face," she said. "I've seen it in your eyes more than once."

"What would you do, Grace," he asked, "if you can't find it?"

She hesitated a moment, then shook her head and said honestly, "I don't know."

They reached Chimney Rock and circled it, so that it was on their right. Fargo kept a sharp eye out, just in case somebody—the Lacys, or whoever was following them earlier in the week—had figured out where they were going and had gotten there ahead of them.

"God," she said, shivering, "this brings back memories."

He knew she meant bad memories, of when her child was stillborn.

"I was in labor when we passed here," she said, thinking back. "I was in pain, and I knew my baby was dying inside me. I knew it."

Her eyes did not fill with tears, however, at this recollection, and suddenly Fargo was filled with doubt. He wasn't sure why, but he was thinking what if they had come all this way not to unearth her stillborn child, but something else that had been buried out here? And if that was the case, what could it be?

"We have to keep going west just a few more miles," she said, "and then we veered to the south and stopped while I . . . delivered the baby."

"All right," he said. "I got us this far, now it's up to you to lead the way."

She looked at him, nodded, and then said, "Very well. Let's go."

       *   *   *

"Here," she said, stopping.

"Here what?"

"This is where we change direction," she said. "I feel it."

"Don't you see any landmarks?"

"After all these years?" she asked. "Can't I just operate on instinct sometime, like you do?"

He wanted to say, "Out here? No." But he didn't.

"All right," he said, instead, "lead on."

When they saw it they both stopped, and then looked at each other.

"That wasn't here then," she said.

"Obviously."

"You talked about landmarks," she said, "there was one. A big rock, almost white, it looked like an egg. I remember one of the men said it looked like God's egg."

Fargo thought that was silly, but he didn't say so.

"But that . . . that wasn't here then," she said, pointing. "Oh my God."

They both stared ahead of them, he surprised but she absolutely shocked that where she thought her baby's burial site should be there was, instead, a town.

14

The town was called, unimaginatively Fargo thought, Big Rock.

"What do we do now?" she asked. "My baby could be . . . under this town."

"Take it easy, Grace," Fargo said. "We'll just have to ride into town and ask a few questions, that's all. Look on the bright side."

"And what's that?" she asked.

"Real beds, bathtubs, hot food," he said. "No more sleeping on the ground for a while."

"But . . . my baby . . ."

He reached out and put a hand on her shoulder.

"We'll find the site, Grace," he said. "We'll find it. Just ride in and find a hotel, for now. All right?"

"Yes," she said, "all right, yes, I'm fine. Let's go, Skye."

They went through the motions of finding the livery, handing their horses over, and then walked to the hotel. As they checked in—getting one room, this time—Fargo asked the desk clerk, a young man in his twenties, how long the town had been there.

"Beats me," he said. "I only been here about a year.

Guess you'll hafta ask somebody who's been around longer than me."

"Okay, thanks," Fargo said.

They took their saddlebags up to their room.

"From the looks of these buildings," Fargo said, looking out the window, "they've been here five or six years. The town could have been here longer, if they started out with temporary buildings, or tents."

"Well, it can't be more than twelve years old," she said. "We know that."

"Are you sure you picked the right spot, Grace?" he asked.

"No, I'm not," she said, gnawing on a nail. "If that white rock was here I'd know. Maybe if we walked around a bit we might see it."

"Walking around seems like a good idea," he said. "We can ask around about the town, find somebody older than that clerk who's been around."

"Can we do it now?"

"Sure," he said, "and we can get something to eat, at the same time."

They walked around for about a half an hour, but didn't see any white rocks like the one Grace described. The town was not very big, and such a rock would probably have stood out.

They stopped a few people and asked about the birth of the town, but nobody seemed to know. Most of them said they'd only come into town in the last few years. And none of them seemed to know who had founded the town. None of them seemed very old, either.

"Maybe you should talk to Mayor Baily," one of them suggested.

"Maybe we should," Fargo agreed. "Thanks."

"Let's go find the mayor," Grace said, after that.

"Grace," Fargo said, "the mayor's not going anywhere, and neither is your baby. Let's get something to eat and settle down a bit."

"All right," she said. "I am finding it a little hard to breathe. It's like I'm holding my breath all the time, you know?"

"Yes, I do know," he said. "Come on, we passed a café a block back."

The café served a decent beef stew, or so the waiter told them. Apparently, he didn't have much to compare it to, but they ate it, anyway. The coffee, at least, was decent.

"Mind if I ask you a question?" Fargo asked the waiter when he came for the dishes.

"About what?" the man asked. He was in his late thirties, certainly old enough to remember the town's origins, if he was there at the time.

"About this town."

"Big Rock?"

Fargo looked at Grace, who shrugged, and then said, "Yes, Big Rock."

"What about it?"

"We were wondering how long it's been here."

"Damned if I know," the waiter said. "I've only been workin' here three years."

"And you never heard anyone talk about the town's origins?"

"The what?"

"When it was founded," Grace said, helpfully.

"Ma'am," the waiter said, "it don't much matter to me when it was found or who found it. I just live and work here."

He took the dirty dishes and walked off.

"Is that how people in the West usually feel about their homes?" she asked.

"I suppose," Fargo said. "What we'll have to do is see if we can't find one of the founders."

"Maybe the mayor is one. What did that fellow say his name was?"

"Baily."

"Right," she said. "We might as well go and find Mayor Baily and see what he knows."

Fargo paid the check, and they left the café to find the mayor.

They found the city hall, which turned out to be a small, wooden, one-story building. On the front window it said MAYOR FELTON BAILY. They walked inside and found a young man of about thirty sitting behind a desk.

"You're the mayor?" Grace asked.

"That's right," Baily said. "A little young for the job, I know, but nobody else wanted it. What can I do for you strangers? Would you like to settle down here?"

"No," Fargo said, "but we do have some questions about your town."

"Ask away," the man said, sitting back in his chair and lacing his fingers behind his head. He made no effort to hide the fact that he was examining Grace with great appreciation.

"Mayor, we're trying to find out how long your town has been here."

"Three years."

"That's all?" Grace asked.

"That's it," he said, "and that's how long I've been mayor of Big Rock."

"Three years," she said.

"Now," the mayor added, "if you're asking how long the buildings have been here, we don't know."

"The buildings?" Fargo asked.

"You see," Baily said, "some of us came here from back East three years ago, looking for someplace to live. Some of us even had California in mind, but we found this place and it was empty. I mean, it was deserted."

"So you moved in?"

He nodded.

"Who named it Big Rock?" Fargo asked.

"Don't know," Baily said. "The name was on everything when we got here, so we kept it."

"Do you know anything about a big white rock, kind of shaped like a giant egg?" Grace asked.

"No, ma'am," Baily said, "can't say I do. We just figured the town was named after Chimney Rock. You know, the big rock."

"Yes," Fargo said, "we know."

It occurred to Fargo that they hadn't seen anyone in town who looked to be over forty, and he mentioned that fact.

"That's about right," Baily said. "See, we were a young crowd when we left the East to come West. I reckon we got one or two people who'll be forty this year, but that's about it."

"Interesting," Fargo said.

"See, that means there's plenty of room for the town to grow," Baily said. "You folks are welcome to settle here, if you like."

"Thanks," Fargo said, "but we're not interested in settling down."

"Why all the questions, then?"

Fargo and Grace exchanged a glance, and it was Grace who said, "We're just curious, Mayor, that's all."

"Thanks for your time," Fargo said, and they left the mayor's storefront office.

"What do we do now?" Grace asked, outside.

"Grace," he said, "there's still a possibility that you missed the mark. Why don't we ride in a widening circle around the town and see if we can't find that white rock of yours?"

"I don't have any better ideas, Skye," she said, touching a hand to her forehead.

"But I think we'll do it tomorrow," Fargo added.

"Why tomorrow?" Grace asked.

"Because you're about to keel over."

"I'm not—"

"And the horses can use the extra rest."

She didn't argue with that.

"Come on," he said, taking her by the arm, "I'll take you back to the hotel."

"What are you going to do?"

"I'm going over to the saloon to have a beer, and just give a listen to what people around here talk about," he said.

"Why?"

"Sometimes people tell you what you want to know when you're not asking them."

He left Grace in the room, looking as if her eyes were going to close any minute. He promised not to be away too long, then left and headed for the saloon. Maybe, after she'd had some rest, she might remember something helpful.

Meanwhile, he could use a beer.

15

Big Rock was far from a busy town, and now Fargo knew why. No town that was barely three years old had time to become busy. When he entered the saloon he was greeted with smiles by the bartender because, other than the two of them, there was only one other man in the place.

"What can I get you, friend?" the bartender asked.

Fargo ordered a beer and studied the man. He decided that this was one of the people the mayor had spoken of, who would probably soon be forty.

"There ya go," the man said. "Nice and cold."

"This town seems to be out in the middle of nowhere," Fargo said around a sip of beer.

"It's gonna grow, though," the man said, confidently.

"I guess so, but where do you get your supplies from?" Fargo asked.

"We send to Magrew for them," the man said. "That's the nearest town."

Fargo wondered if anyone in Magrew would know when this town was built, or if anyone would remember a white rock shaped like an egg.

"Where's that?"

"North of here about fifty miles."

"Long haul."

"Closest town," the man said again.

Fargo wondered if between here and Magrew there wasn't that rock.

"What are you lookin' for, friend?" the bartender asked.

"A big white rock, shaped like an egg."

The bartender thought a minute then said, "That don't ring no bells with me a-tall."

"Do you know anyone who might remember it?"

"Well," he said, "this town's pretty young, but there's a bunch of old-timers livin' in Magrew. You might wanna go there and ask around."

That made sense to Fargo. Might as well go where there were some older people with longer memories.

He finished his beer and said, "Much obliged."

"If you're goin' to Magrew you'll want to remember somethin'."

"What's that?"

"You might run into Cheyenne, or Pawnee."

"Friendly?"

"We trade with the Pawnee, some."

"And the Cheyenne?"

"Kill ya just as soon as look at ya."

"Thanks," Fargo said, "I will remember that."

On the way back to the hotel Fargo was trying to decide how to play this with Grace. He finally decided to go ahead and tell her about the Indians. After that he was going to suggest that she remain in Big Rock while he went to Magrew to ask questions. If he ran into Indians along the way he'd be much better off alone than with a woman along. He'd have to make her see it that way.

* * *

"I'm not staying here alone," she said, when he made his proposal.

"Grace," he said, "if we run into the Cheyenne—hell, or even the Pawnee—the chances are they're going to want you."

"You'll protect me," she replied. "You said you'd protect me."

"And I will," he said, "but not against ten or twelve Cheyenne braves. I'll get killed and you'll be taken as a squaw."

"There was a woman in the wagon train I was with," she said. "She'd been taken by the Indians, and her face had been painted. It was something that wouldn't come off, and so she had to live among the white people with these . . . markings on her face. They made her stand out."

"What's your point?"

"She wanted to go back to them," she said. "How badly could they have treated her?"

"Grace, do you really want to find out the answer to that question?"

She firmed her jaw and stood up from the bed she'd been seated on.

"Skye Fargo, I'm paying you, and I'm going with you. If you don't take me, I'll follow you. How long do you think I'll last out there alone?"

"Not long," he said. "You're a stubborn woman, Grace."

"What if you come to that rock between here and there . . . wherever . . ."

"Magrew."

"Fine, Magrew. I want to be with you."

"All right," he said, pointing his finger at her, "but if and when I tell you to shoot that rifle . . . *at* somebody . . . I expect you to do it."

"If it will get me closer to my baby," she said, "I will."

"Never mind closer to your baby," Fargo said. "It will keep us alive!"

Fargo decided that they would leave for Magrew first thing in the morning. Until then they'd just have to pass the time any way they could. At the moment sex was out of the question. He was still a little peeved with her, and she with him for wanting to leave her behind. He decided to go back to the saloon.

"I'm going to do some shopping," she said.

"That's fine," he said. "I'll meet you back here around seven and we'll have something to eat together."

"Fine," she said.

"Fine," he said.

They left the hotel together and went their separate ways.

The bartender greeted Fargo with smiles again, and now there were two other men in the place. Fargo couldn't tell if one of them was the same as the one who was there earlier. He ordered another beer.

"On the house," the bartender said.

"How come?"

"Second one's on the house," the man said. "You left without your second one before."

"Thanks."

"Find out what you wanted to?" the bartender asked.

"Not really."

"Goin' to Magrew?"

"Why do you ask?"

"I thought of somebody you could talk to, might help you out."

"Oh? Who?"

"His name's Jonas Beech. Old-timer who runs the general store there. Should of thought of him before. We buy most of our supplies from him. He's been around here forever. Must be close to seventy, ol' Jonas."

"I appreciate it," Fargo said. "Jonas Beech."

"That's right. Tell him Ray sent you, from Big Rock. Chances are he'd talk to you anyways, but it won't hurt to drop my name."

"Thanks, I will."

Two more men came in and stopped at the far end of the bar. Ray went down to wait on them, so Fargo worked on his beer. He finally had the name of somebody to talk to. A man in his seventies should remember something— providing he *could* still remember things.

Ray came back and asked, "Another one?"

"No, thanks. Listen, this Jonas, does he have, uh—" Fargo was trying to think of a way to ask the question that wouldn't be insulting.

"All his brains? Sure does. Jonas is as sharp as a tack. If anybody will know anything, it's him."

"Thanks again, Ray."

"Sure thing, Mr.—?"

"Skye Fargo," Fargo replied, and left without noticing whether or not Ray the bartender recognized the name.

* * *

Fargo made one more stop he should have made earlier, at the sheriff's office. When he entered there was a man standing by a gun rack, looking as if he'd just put a rifle back in place.

"Help ya?" he asked.

"Are you the sheriff?"

"That's me," the man said.

He pushed on the rifle one more time, making sure it was firmly in place, and then turned to face Fargo. The movement revealed the star on his chest. It also gave away the fact that he was not yet thirty, and might even have been closer to twenty-five. From the looks of his jaw, he didn't have to shave every day yet.

"Sheriff Sam Brod's my name. What can I do for you, Mr.—?"

"My name's Fargo, Skye Fargo."

If the name registered with the lawman, he didn't show it.

"What can I do for you, Mr. Fargo?"

"Well," Fargo began to explain, "I just got into town a little while ago and it looked like an interesting little place."

"It is," Brod said. "We think it's gonna outgrow Magrew, pretty soon."

"Really?"

"Sure thing," the man said proudly.

"Hasn't Magrew been around a long time?"

"Sure has."

"And this town is how old?"

"Few years."

"I understand a lot of the citizens came from back East," Fargo said. "Did you come with them?"

"Nope," Brod said. "Fact is, I got hired just last year."

"I see."

"I know what you're thinkin'." The man walked around behind his desk and sat down.

"You do?"

"That I'm a little young to be a sheriff."

"Well . . ."

"I did some deputy work here and there, and then I heard that Big Rock was lookin' for a sheriff. I applied for the job, and got it."

"Well, you must've deserved it."

"Fact is," Brod said, "nobody else wanted it. I've earned it, though, over the past year."

"I'm sure you have, Sheriff. Uh, listen. I'm going to be riding to Magrew tomorrow. You got any advice for me? about the ride, I mean?"

"Just watch out for the Cheyenne," Brod said. "The Pawnee, they might not bother you, but the Cheyenne'll kill you on the spot."

"Much obliged, then."

"Gonna be ridin' alone?"

"Uh, no, as a matter of fact, I won't. Well—"

"Who's gonna be ridin' with you?" the lawman asked. "It's always good to ride in twos, or more."

"Just one other rider," Fargo said. "Well, thanks for your help, Sheriff."

"I only got one more piece of advice for you, Mr. Fargo," the sheriff said as Fargo headed for the door.

"And that would be, Sheriff?"

"Make sure you don't take any women out there with you," Brod said. "The Cheyenne are always lookin' for white women."

"I'll keep that in mind," Fargo said, and left the office before the lawman could ask him any more questions.

16

By the time they finished their meal together, Fargo and Grace were ready to be civil to each other again.

"How about a walk?" he asked.

"I'd like to walk off the meal and take a look at the town," she said. Earlier she'd been too busy questioning people, and looking for the big white rock to notice what the town looked like.

They left the hotel and started walking. People passed them along the way, most of them offering some sort of greeting.

"These look like your kind of people," Fargo said.

"What kind is that?"

"Civilized people who came here from the East to live," he answered. "Obviously, most of them like it."

"I don't know if I could live here," she said, "knowing that there are Indians out there who would kill me as soon as look at me."

"They'd kill me," he said. "They'd take you captive."

"You're telling the truth, I know," she said, "but you're also trying to scare me into staying here while you go to Magrew. It's not going to work."

"Speaking of Magrew," he said, "I got the name of somebody we can talk to there."

He told her about Jonas Beech.

"He sounds perfect," she said. "He should know everything that's gone on here for years."

"We hope," Fargo said.

They walked to the end of town, then crossed the street for the walk back.

"It seems so peaceful, and nice," she said. "Not at all like Council Bluffs."

Fargo knew Grace would be in for a big shock if he took her to some real western towns and she saw how truly untamed many of them still were. To her, Council Bluffs had been a rowdy place.

"You know," he said, "there are some civilized places to live out here."

"Like where?"

"Well, Denver, San Francisco—"

"That's California," she said.

"So?"

"So that's not the West."

He laughed.

"You can't get any further west without ending up in the ocean."

"You know what I mean."

"No, what do you mean?"

"I mean the Wild West that you read about in the penny dreadfuls."

"Those things are published back East," Fargo said, "by people who have no idea what it's like out here. You've been out here long enough to know you can't judge the West by reading those."

"Perhaps," she said, "but I've also ready newspaper accounts."

"Oh, and those are always true," he said, rolling his eyes.

"Back East they are," she said. "The newspapers there are very reputable."

"There's no such thing as a reputable newspaper," he said, "or newspaperman."

"You sound as if you're speaking from personal experience."

"I am."

"You've had some bad experiences with newspapers?"

"I have."

"And you judge them all by that?"

"I've had the same experience with enough of them to do that, yes."

"Well . . ." she said, as if not sure how to respond to that. "I guess I can't argue with your experience."

At times Fargo found Grace to be very naive, which he found odd. She struck him as an intelligent woman and—as she would put it—certainly civilized, but her outlook was sometimes odd for someone her age.

"It doesn't really matter," he said. "Some people believe everything they read, and some people don't. I think we should get back to the hotel."

"All right."

Instead of completing an entire circuit of the town, that's what they did.

Back in the room all questions ceased to be asked, or even thought of. They tumbled into bed together and lost themselves in each other for the night. When Fargo was inside of Grace he didn't think about her baby, or if it really was a baby she was looking to dig up. He didn't worry about anyone following them, or the Cheyenne, or the Pawnee, or any of that. In bed, they were just a man and a woman and everything else was forgotten, at least for the night. . . .

When Fargo woke up the next morning Grace was all over him, which was not something he was about to complain about. Her hand was on his penis, tickling it and teasing it to life, while at the same time bringing him awake. Both he and his penis were ready at the same time. He reached down, put his hands under her arms, and pulled her up onto him. She slid down his pole with her eyes closed and her head back and began to grind herself down on him so that he couldn't possibly get any deeper into her.

"Ooooh yes," she moaned, pressing her palms down onto his hard belly, lifting herself and then bringing herself down on him, and then *grinding* again. "Oh, Skye. My God, yes, yes, yes . . ."

He found himself wondering if she'd ever said, "My God," while having sex with her preacher husband, but the question—and all others—quickly fled from his mind as she leaned over and fed her breasts to him. He took one nipple into his mouth and sucked it, then the other, held the breasts in his hands while he kissed and suckled them and she moaned appreciatively.

She sat straight up as the time came near, closing her eyes and arching her back, giving herself up to the wonderful sensations that were coursing through her body.

"Oh, yes, oooh, I feel it, Skye, I feel . . . oh, oh, ooooooh . . ." She groaned aloud as the sensations began to center themselves. She felt as if her crotch were on fire and she rode him harder and faster and he tried to stay with her, tried not to explode until he felt her trembling, until her insides began to spasm and suck at him, until she began to bounce on him uncontrollably and then when she gasped and suddenly just stopped on him he erupted inside of her. . . .

They had breakfast in the hotel the next morning after checking out. There were other people in the dining room, some guests of the hotel and others just townspeople, and many of them greeted them when they entered.

"I'm from the East," she said, "and even I'm not used to this."

"I'm not, either," Fargo said. "The people in this town seem extraordinarily friendly."

The waiter took their order with a smile and delivered the food the same way.

"Hope you folks enjoy your food," he said.

They did, but they both left the hotel feeling as if they were somehow being targeted.

"Do you think they're this nice to everyone?" she asked him.

"I don't know," Fargo said, "but I can tell you this. Having people be *too* nice to you feels kind of . . . suspicious."

"I know what you mean."

They walked to the livery to collect their horses for the ride to Magrew.

"Grace, you've got one more chance to change your mind," he said as they walked their horses outside.

"About what?"

"About staying behind."

"I already told you—"

"Okay," he said, holding his hands up, "don't bite my head off."

"We were just talking about how . . . odd this place is," she reminded him. "I want to leave."

"All right," he said. "I can't say that I blame you for that. Let's go."

They mounted up and rode through town and kept going west, a route that would take them to Magrew and—they hoped—toward their final goal.

"How far did they say Magrew was?" she asked, after they'd ridden a couple of hours.

"About fifty miles or so."

Fargo knew that at a good pace, with a good horse, he could do fifty miles in a day. He didn't know if that applied to Grace and her horse, though. She hadn't complained in some time about soreness, and so far her horse had kept up, but he hadn't pushed them at all, and he didn't think he needed to now. If they camped the night somewhere and got to Magrew the next day, that was fine with him.

They could still see Chimney Rock behind them and some hills around it, but ahead of them the ground was flat and hard. That was why Fargo was able to see the riders ahead of them.

"Son of a bitch," he said.

"What?"

He reined in and she followed.

"Riders."

She looked ahead, squinting, and was able to make them out, as well.

"What are they doing?"

"Just sitting their horses, waiting."

"Who are they?"

"Don't know."

She squinted more.

"Could it be the Lacys, from Council Bluffs?"

"Could be," he said. "Looks like . . . four of them."

"How'd they get ahead of us?"

"Well," Fargo said, "they're not that smart, but there is a fourth rider. When they lost us he might have decided that Chimney Rock was a good point to triangulate on."

"And he was right."

"Looks like."

"So he was smart."

"And smart men are dangerous."

"What do we do?" she asked. "Change direction again?"

"It's too late for that," he said. "They're moving now."

"Should we run?"

He looked around.

"Where would we go?" he asked. "There's not much cover out here."

She looked around, also, but in more of a panicky way.

"Skye? What do we do?"

"Well," he said, "for want of something better, let's try riding to meet them, and talking to them."

"But . . . won't they just kill us?"

"I think," he said, "they want to know why we're out here, Grace. They haven't ridden all this way just to kill us. They could have tried that right in Council Bluffs."

"And when we tell them it's because of a dead baby?" she asked.

124

"It might be wise," he replied, "if by the time they reached us, we came up with a different story."

They rode forward for a few moments, as the four riders came toward them, and then Fargo said, "Why doesn't this surprise me?"

"What is it?"

"It is the Lacys," he said.

"And the fourth man?"

"Somebody I recognize."

"You know him?"

"Not really," he said. "I just saw him around Council Bluffs, sort of watching me."

"Who is it?"

"His name is Billy Denver," Fargo said, "and he fancies himself a gunman."

"So what does he want?"

"I guess we'll be finding that out . . . real soon."

17

As the riders got closer to each other, Fargo said to Grace, "Take out your rifle."

"What?"

"Your rifle," he said, again. "I want you to hold it like you know how to use it."

She picked up the rifle and held it awkwardly.

"Just tuck it into the crook of your arm and hold it," he said, carefully. "I don't think you'll have to use it—not yet, anyway."

"How will I know—"

"If I start shooting," he said, "you start shooting. Just pick one of the men out—one of the Lacy brothers—and keep your eyes on him."

"Why?"

"I want him to think that he's the one you'll shoot," Fargo said.

"All right."

"And let me do all the talking."

"All right," she said, again.

Fargo took his rifle out and held it across his lap as they approached. When they got within about twenty feet of each other they all stopped.

"Fargo," Billy Denver said.

"Hello, Denver," Fargo said. "What are you doing with these three losers?"

"Who you callin'—" one of the Lacys started, but Denver cut him off.

"Shut up, Paul."

"But—"

"Shut up, Paul," Les Lacy said.

"We're payin' him—" Paul started, but a sharp look from his older brother finally quieted him.

"You're on their payroll, Denver?" Fargo asked.

"Why not?" Denver asked. "You're on hers, aren't you?"

"True enough."

"Fargo," Denver said, "you and me ought to be able to figure something out here."

"Like what?"

"According to these fellas," Denver said, "the lady has a lot of money, and has something valuable buried somewhere out here."

"Is that a fact?"

"Well, I don't know if it's a fact," Denver said. "It's what these three have told me, though."

"And you believe them?"

"You believe what she's been tellin' you?"

"Sure, why not?"

"Well, why shouldn't I believe them?"

"Because the three of them are morons," Fargo said.

"Actually," Denver said, "I think two of them are morons."

Les Lacy preened, figuring he was the one Denver had left out.

"The other one's just an idiot," Denver finished.

127

Les deflated, but kept quiet.

"Now," Denver said, "suppose you tell me what the lady's got buried out here that brought you, her, and these three all this way?"

Fargo decided to tell the truth. "A baby."

Denver hesitated, then said, "What?"

"A dead baby."

"Why would anyone want to dig up a dead baby?" Denver asked.

"To give it the proper burial it didn't get twelve years ago, when it was stillborn."

"Still what?" Paul asked.

"Born dead, you moron," Denver said.

"Oh."

"Now shut up!"

Paul fell silent.

"That's what she told you?" Denver asked.

"That's right."

"And you believe her?"

"Yes."

"Why? Because you're sleepin' with her?"

"Is that why you believe these three?"

That got Denver's back up for a moment, but then he saw what Fargo was trying to do.

"Don't try to rile me, Fargo," the gunman said. "I don't rile easy. You're one man facin' four, with only a woman to back you up. I want some straight answers."

"I've been giving you straight answers, Denver," Fargo said.

"Then maybe I should talk to the lady? She seems to have you buffaloed."

"The lady's not talking."

"Why not?"

"That's what she's paying me for."

"I thought she was paying you for protection?"

"That, too."

"You gonna protect her from the four of us?"

"If lead starts flying," Fargo said, "at least two of you are going to go down, and probably the two of us. When she's dead, you'll never find out what she buried."

Denver studied Fargo for a few moments, then spread his hands and smiled.

"Who's talkin' about makin' lead fly?" he asked.

"There's nothin' here for you, Denver," Fargo said. "The lady wants her dead baby, that's all."

Denver brought his hands back to his sides, controlling his horse with his knees and legs.

"All right," Denver said, "for the sake of argument let's say she buried a dead baby. What about the money she has?"

"It's in the bank."

"What?"

"She didn't go near the bank in Council Bluffs, Billy," Les Lacy said. "We know that."

"Not the bank in Council Bluffs," Fargo said.

"Then which one?" Denver asked.

"Big Rock."

"That one-horse town?"

"It had a bank," Fargo said, with a shrug.

"He's lyin'," Paul said.

"Maybe," Denver said.

"If I'm not," Fargo said, "we could all be dying for nothing out here."

"Talkin' about dyin' again," Denver said. "Why do you have it in your head I'm here to kill you, Fargo?"

"Because I think you've been waitin' to try, Billy," Fargo said. "You were just waitin' for someone to pay you to do it."

"Billy," Les said, warningly, "don't kill the woman until we find out if they're lyin'. If that money's in the bank—"

"We'll just go take it out," Denver said, "along with whoever else's happens to be in there."

"We gonna rob a bank?" Paul asked.

"Shut up, Paul," Denver said.

Fargo didn't know which Lacy brother Grace had fixed her eyes on, but he was willing to bet it was the older one, Les. The middle one had remained quiet, while Paul was the one everyone kept telling to shut up. Fargo's first target was going to have to be Billy Denver. After that it would be every man—and woman—for themselves.

Then somebody else took a hand in the game.

Suddenly, both Fargo and Denver heard something.

"Quiet!" Denver said, to everyone. "Fargo?"

"I hear it," Fargo said.

"What is it?" Les Lacy asked.

"Ponies," Denver said.

"Unshod," Fargo said.

"Lots of them," Denver added.

"If they're Cheyenne we're in trouble," Fargo said. "Pawnee, and we have a chance."

"Shit," Denver said. "Indians. I *hate* Indians. Can't tell them apart."

"Where are they comin' from?" Les Lacy asked, looking around as his brothers were doing, wide-eyed.

"Don't panic," Denver said. "If you do—"

"I'm gettin' out of here!" Paul shouted, and kicked his heels into his horse.

"No!" Denver said.

But he was too late. All three of the Lacy boys bolted and started to ride before they knew what direction the Indians were coming from. As it turned out they rode right into the arms of about fifteen Indian braves. It didn't matter if they were Cheyenne or Pawnee, because the three white men started shooting first, and whatever tribe the Indians were from, they had no recourse but to fire back, cutting all three brothers down.

"Fargo," Grace said, her voice frightened.

"Just sit tight, Grace," Fargo said.

"Those fools might have just got us killed," Denver said.

"Maybe not," Fargo said. "We'll have to wait and see."

Denver turned his horse so he could stand with Fargo and Grace. The three of them watched as the Indians dismounted and relieved the three dead men of their valuables. Only after they were done did they all look up at the remaining three riders.

"They're gonna want the woman," Denver said.

"Maybe," Fargo said.

"The only chance we have of gettin' out of this alive," the gunman said, "is to give her to them."

"That's not an option," Fargo said.

"I'm not dyin' for her," Denver said.

"If you try to give her to them," Fargo said, "I'll kill you myself."

"Big deal," Billy Denver said, "what do I care who kills me, you or them? Dead is dead."

Fargo hated to admit it, but he had a point.

"Fargo?" Grace said.

"Yeah?"

"Are they . . . Pawnee?"

"I don't know yet, Grace," he said.

"I sure hope they are," Denver said. "If they are, they'll trade for her. If they're Cheyenne, they'll just kill us and take her."

18

As they got closer, Fargo had to admit he didn't know if they were Pawnee or Cheyenne. They weren't wearing warpaint, though, and had only killed the Lacy brothers when fired upon first. There was still a good chance they were Pawnee.

"Should we throw down our guns?" Grace asked. "Show them we're not a threat?"

"No!" Fargo said, stopping her before she could do it. "It's better to hold on to our guns and show them we're not afraid."

"I agree," Billy Denver said. "The Indians respect courage, ma'am. I suggest that's all you show them."

"Do the same thing you did with the Lacys, Grace," Fargo said. "Pick one of these braves and just keep staring at him."

Finally, the Indians came close enough to smell and stopped. There were eleven of them, and one sat his horse ahead of the other ten, presumably the leader. Fargo could see that he only had eyes for Grace. After a few moments of drinking her in, though, he switched his gaze to the two men.

They all stared at each other for a while, and then the brave said something in his native tongue. When neither

Fargo nor Denver replied, he waved and another brave rode up beside him.

"Katonka want to know if you were with those men," the interpreter said.

"We were not," Fargo said, conveniently forgetting that Denver had, indeed, been with the Lacys. "They were our enemies. We thank you for killing them for us."

"We are Pawnee," the interpreter said. "We only kill when we are attacked."

"That is good," Fargo said.

"Or when we see something we want."

"Oh Lord," Grace said, under her breath.

"Katonka want to know whose woman she is," the brave said, pointing at Grace.

"She is my woman," Fargo said.

The interpreter filled Katonka in on this, and then listened to the reply.

"Katonka say he trade many ponies for her."

"We have horses," Fargo said. "I don't need any more."

"Three ponies."

"No."

He waited while his reply was interpreted.

"Katonka say he trade weapons."

"I have weapons."

"Three fine rifles."

"No."

The Indians had a brief conference.

"Skins."

"I don't need skins."

"Three fine skins."

"No."

Another conference ensued, during which Katonka seemed to become agitated.

"He say what you take for woman?"

"Tell Katonka I would not trade my woman for anything," Fargo said. "She is a poor cook, does not keep my lodge clean, and has not bore me any sons, but I still wish to keep her."

"Hey—" Grace said.

"If he thinks you're the perfect wife," Fargo said to her in a low voice, "he'll want you even more. Just keep quiet."

"I was not with those men," Billy Denver said to the brave, "and I am not with these people. I will move on and leave you to your trading."

As he started to move his horse forward, the Pawnee who had rifles—Spencers, from the looks of them—pointed them at him.

"Do not move," the interpreter said.

Denver reined in his horse and raised his hands in a supplicating gesture.

"I only wish to move on," he said.

"You will wait."

Denver shrugged and folded his arms across his chest so as not to look menacing.

The interpreter looked back at Fargo.

"Katonka say you are not being fair," the brave said. "He is willing to trade anything for the woman."

"Tell Katonka I don't think he is being fair," Fargo said. "I want to keep her."

"Why?" Katonka asked, through the interpreter. "If

she is such a poor squaw, why do you want to keep her?"

Fargo shrugged and said, "I have had her for a long time. I am used to her."

"Katonka will trade you three squaws who will cook good, clean good, and give you many sons."

"No," Fargo said.

Katonka became angry, then.

"Katonka is angry," the brave said.

"I can see that," Fargo said.

"I think he's been more than patient," Billy Denver said, to whoever would listen.

"Katonka say you just fight for her."

"Fargo—" Grace said.

"Tell Katonka I will fight him for her, but if I win, you will let us go."

"All three of us," Denver threw in.

"All three of us."

There was a conference, and then Katonka waved and three braves came forward.

"Katonka say he offer you three ponies, three rifles, three skins, and three squaws and you say no. Katonka say you fight for three people, so you must fight three braves."

"That's not fair!" Grace shouted.

"I will fight your three braves," Fargo said, "but since I cannot use three ponies at once, or three rifles at once, or three squaws at once—"

"That's debatable," Denver said.

"—I will fight the three braves one at a time, one right after the other."

The brave relayed this to Katonka, who thought it over and then nodded.

"Done," the brave said.

"Let's dismount," Fargo said to Grace and Denver.

"Aren't you going to help him?" Grace demanded of Denver.

"He's the one who wants to keep you," Denver said. "I would have taken the three squaws or ponies."

"He saved your life by not telling them that you were with the Lacy brothers."

"Well," Denver said, after a moment, "I do have to admit that you have a point there. All right, I'll help."

"Good," she said.

"I'll give advice."

"Thanks," Fargo said, removing his gunbelt and hanging it on his saddle, then rolling up his sleeves.

"Weapons?" Fargo asked the interpreter.

"No weapons," the brave said. "Bare hands."

That suited Fargo. No matter how good he might have been with a knife, an Indian would have been better.

The three braves were slightly different in size, each a bit larger than the one before. First, the smaller one came forward. He was Fargo's size, but with more bulk, which led Fargo to believe that he would be the quicker of the two. He'd have to use that to his advantage.

"I think you'll be quicker than he is," Denver said. "Use that to your advantage."

Fargo stared at the man and then said, "That's good advice. Thank you, Billy."

Denver took Grace by the arm and moved her back, away from the action.

"I hope you appreciate what we're doin' for you," he said.

"What *you're* doing for me?" she demanded.

Denver frowned and looked away.

19

Fargo moved forward a bit then stopped, deciding to make the brave come to him. They were fighting in a circle formed by the other ten braves. Tentatively, Denver and Grace also moved into the circle.

Fargo kept his arms loose at his sides and waited. He felt the brave would become impatient and rush him eventually, and that's what happened. As the man came forward Fargo suddenly dropped and, using his legs, tripped the brave, who fell onto his face. Fargo quickly leaped on the man's back and captured his head in the crook of his left arm. With his right hand he exerted pressure, threatening to snap the man's neck but stopping just short. He used his forearm to cut off the man's wind, and before he knew it the brave went limp beneath him. He released the man before he could die from lack of air, and stood up.

Grace started to applaud, and when the other braves looked at her she stopped.

"He got lucky there," Denver said.

"Lucky? He was wonderful."

"Let's see how he makes out with the second one."

Fargo turned and, as two other braves dragged away the unconscious one, the second man stepped forward.

This one was not only bulkier than he, but several inches taller. He didn't think he could hope for this man to make the same mistake, so he decided to be the aggressor this time.

He approached the bigger brave, who had obviously learned from watching the first fight. He held back and waited, then began moving slowly forward, shuffling his feet, keeping his arms loose at his sides. Suddenly, Fargo darted in and shot out a left that landed squarely on the brave's nose. It seemed to burst in a spray of red, which ran down the lower portion of the man's face and dripped off his chest. His eyes immediately began to tear and he didn't even see Fargo step in to launch a right hand that connected and almost tore his head off. Fargo was sure that he could feel the man's jaw snap, and the Indian's eyes slid up into his head and he dropped to the ground in a boneless sprawl.

This time Grace applauded and did not let the glares from the other Indians deter her.

"You can't call that luck," she said to Denver.

"No," he said, "I call that a helluva a right hand. If we get out of this alive, I wonder if Fargo would let me manage him in a prizefighting career."

Fargo backed away as two braves came forward to drag away the second unconscious Pawnee brave.

Then the third brave stepped into the circle. He was a full head taller than Fargo and even without an ounce of fat on his body, must have weighed close to three hundred pounds.

"My God!" Grace said.

"He is a big one," Denver said. "I wonder if Fargo can take him."

This brave looked as if he were chiseled out of granite. He stared at Fargo, who stared back, seemingly unfazed by the sheer size of the man. In truth he would rather have faced a grizzly bear at that moment, although there really wasn't much difference between the two, except for the hair on the bear.

"Mr. Denver?" Grace said.

"Yes, ma'am?"

"Would you do me a great favor?"

"What would that be, ma'am?"

"If Fargo is killed by this huge Indian," she said, "and since you still have your gun, would you shoot me?"

"Rather than let you fall into their hands, ma'am," Denver said, "and since they're probably gonna kill me anyway, it would be my pleasure."

"Thank you."

They turned their attention to the two men in the circle. Denver realized that with the two braves Fargo had already dispatched, and the one he was preparing to fight now, there were only eight left in the circle. Between them, in a surprise attack, he and Fargo just might be able to get them out of this situation.

While everyone was watching the two men, Denver backed up a bit until he could take Fargo's gun from the holster that was hanging on his saddle, tuck it into his belt, and then move back into the circle.

"Ma'am?"

"Yes?"

"Can you use that rifle that's on your saddle?" he asked.

"Uh, yes . . . why?"

"Because when I start shooting," he said, "I want you

to grab for it and shoot the nearest Indian. Have you got that?"

"Yes sir."

"Can you do that?"

Grace swallowed and said, "Yes sir."

"Good," he said. "On my signal, then."

"A-all right."

"Get him, Fargo!" Denver yelled, and everyone stopped and looked at him, including Fargo and the huge brave.

"Sorry," he said.

As they all turned their attention back to the fight, Denver said to Grace, "I wonder of any of these braves are gamblers?"

"You want to bet on Fargo?"

"Are you crazy?" he asked. "I'd bet my last dime on the big Indian."

Fargo circled the huge brave, studying him for a weak point. He had been lucky, he knew, to do away with the other two so easily. As a result he was not that winded, but he was at a distinct size disadvantage and he wasn't at all sure that speed could make up for that.

The two combatants circled each other warily, and Fargo decided that the brave was not going to come to him. He darted in quickly and flicked out his left, hoping for the same result as with the second brave. Instead, this huge brave moved quickly and batted his hand away. Fargo threw a right hand, then, and the same thing happened. The brave swatted it away as if it were a fly.

So much for any speed advantage he might have had.

The third time he threw a punch the brave pushed it aside, crouched just a bit, and hit Fargo in the ribs. The blow shook him, and he was sure it had probably cracked a rib. He backed away quickly, favoring that side, and tried to rethink his strategy.

They circled each other and Fargo was only able to see one other possible advantage that he had: the fact that he was wearing boots, and the brave was barefoot. In being able to employ this advantage, though, he was going to have to get close.

He shuffled forward a bit, feinted with a left, and then swung his right. This time it landed right on the brave's jaw, but it didn't faze the man. Fargo was not sure he even saw the big man blink.

"Uh-oh," he heard Billy Denver say.

Obviously, this man could take a punch, because that right hand had done more damage to Fargo than to him. Fargo decided not to use that hand again, because he was sure that next time it would break. He was hoping that Billy Denver was coming up with a plan to get them out of this, and he thought he'd probably need his right hand for it.

He backed away again, then stepped forward and launched a kick that was meant for the big Indian's balls. The brave saw it coming and brought his thigh up. Fargo's foot hit the thigh, which felt like a tree trunk. Instead of stepping back, though, Fargo brought his boot heel down on the brave's bare foot. He knew he heard bones crack and the big man's eyes widened, his mouth opened, and he fell onto his ass, grabbing for his foot.

"Fargo!" Denver shouted.

Fargo turned in time to see his gun flying through the air toward him. By the time he caught it Denver was already firing. Fargo turned, looking for Katonka or the interpreter. When he spotted them, he fired at them while they scrambled to bring their rifles up. Fargo heard rifle fire and hoped that it was Grace, doing her part.

He fired first at braves who had rifles, leaving the others for last. Some of the braves, in bringing their rifles up, fired them prematurely into the ground, and the air was filled with the sound of shots.

The Pawnee braves who didn't have rifles tried to bring an arrow to their bow, or bring up a lance they were holding, but Denver had stepped back and retrieved his own rifle from his saddle. He dropped his empty handgun to the ground and began firing the rifle as quickly as he could.

When Fargo ran out of bullets he had no choice but to charge at the remaining braves. What he didn't account for was the huge fallen brave who, while he couldn't stand on his broken foot, was able to grab Fargo by the legs and drag him to the ground. Fargo scrambled to turn but the brave's arms, like two huge pythons, wrapped themselves around him and he found himself in a bear hug that was threatening to crush his ribs into powder. He did the only thing he could do. He brought his head back, striking the brave on the bridge of the nose with the back of his head. When the man's hold did not yield he did this again, and again, and again, until the back of his head was soaked with blood and the man's arms fell away. He scrambled away, got to his feet, and regarded the brave, whose face was a mass of blood. The man was not out, though, so Fargo stepped forward and very deliberately kicked the man in the head.

That was when he realized that all the shooting had stopped.

20

Fargo sat up and looked around. Grace came running over to him, her rifle in her hand.

"Are you all right?"

He got to his feet and looked around. All around them there were Pawnee on the ground.

"Would they have let us go?" she asked him. "If you'd won?"

"I don't know," he said.

"We couldn't take that chance," Billy Denver said, coming over.

"I . . . killed two of them, I think," she said.

"It had to be done, Grace," Fargo said.

"But . . . they might have let us go."

"You can't justify or not justify this, Grace," he said, putting his hand on her shoulder. "We did what we had to do. That's all."

He looked at Denver.

"Are they all dead?"

"All but two," Denver said.

"Which two?"

"The big one. You kicked him in the head and knocked him out. I don't know if he'll ever come to, but he's still breathing."

"And who else?"

"The one who spoke English," Denver said. "I think we should finish them both."

"No," Fargo said. "Leave them."

Denver looked as if he was going to argue, but then shrugged and busied himself ejecting the spent shells from his gun, reloading and holstering it.

"I was pretty impressed, Fargo," he said.

"I got lucky."

"That's what he said," Grace told him.

"Still," Denver said, "pretty impressive—all of it. If you hadn't caught that gun when I tossed it . . . who knows?"

"What's it going to be between you and me, Denver?" Fargo asked. He had reloaded his own gun and now holstered it.

"Well," Denver said, "those three were going to pay me, and now they're dead. I'm not on anyone's payroll."

"So what will you do?" Grace asked.

"I think the three of us should stick together," Denver said, "at least until we reach another town."

"Magrew," Fargo said. "We're halfway there."

"Magrew it is, then," the gunman said.

"Are the horses all right?" Fargo asked. "There was a lot of lead flying around."

"The horses are fine."

"We should go, then, before more of them show up," Fargo said.

"We should kill these two," Denver said. "If others do show up they'll tell them what happened."

"I'm against it," Fargo said.

"Well," Denver said, "I ain't gonna argue with you."

They walked to the horses and Fargo helped Grace up into her saddle. Denver mounted up, but Fargo hesitated.

"What is it?" Grace asked.

"I wonder . . ." he said. "Give me a minute."

He walked over to where the interpreter was lying. He'd been shot in the shoulder, and his eyes were clouded with pain.

"If you had left us alone," Fargo said, "this would not have happened."

"You are . . . a mighty . . . warrior," the man said to him.

"Help me, then."

"How can I . . . help you?"

"A big white rock," Fargo said, "smooth, like a giant egg. Do you know it?"

"An . . . egg?"

"A rock," Fargo said, again, "shaped like an egg. Have you ever seen it?"

The man thought a moment, then said, "Yes."

"Where?"

"A short ride . . . into the setting sun."

"West," Fargo said. "Thank you."

"You will not . . . kill me?"

"No," Fargo said. "I will leave you here for your people to find."

The brave nodded, then closed his eyes and passed out.

Fargo walked back to where Grace and Denver were waiting on their horses.

"What happened?" she asked. "What did he tell you?"

"Where the big white rock is," Fargo said, mounting up.

"Where?"

"Between here and Magrew," he said. "We would have come to it, eventually. You were off by better than twenty miles, Grace."

"Well," she said, "it has been twelve years."

"Yes," Fargo said, "it has."

"What's with this white rock?" Denver asked.

"You'll find out," Fargo said. "We all will. Come on, let's go."

"I see it!" Grace shouted excitedly, barely half an hour later. "I see it!"

"I see it, too," Fargo said.

She kicked her heels into her horse's ribs and galloped toward the white rock.

"What is that thing?" Denver asked.

"A landmark," Fargo said.

"For what?"

"A grave."

Denver opened his mouth to ask another question but Fargo sent the Ovaro after Grace. He heard Denver's horse coming after them.

By the time he reached the white rock, Grace was off her horse and was touching it. He reined in, grounded the reins, and walked over to her.

"Grace."

"This is it," she said, running her hands over the smooth surface over and over.

"Grace."

"This is it."

"I know it is," he said. "Grace!" He grabbed her by the shoulders and turned her around. Denver reached them by that time.

"Where is the site from here, Grace?"

"Wait," she said, "give me a minute."

He released her and she turned to face the rock again. Then she turned so that it was at her back, and she could see Chimney Rock in the distance.

"Of course," she said. "How could I have made that mistake?"

"A twenty-mile mistake," Fargo pointed out.

"It's this way," she said. "We have to find soft ground."

She led the way and Fargo followed. Behind him Billy Denver dismounted and followed along, also.

Grace walked as if she were pacing it off, and then suddenly stopped.

"Here," she said, her hands held so that the palms faced the ground. "Right here . . . somewhere."

Fargo looked down. The ground was hard. He looked around and saw a few spots where it wasn't so hard, where a hole might have been dug that was large enough for a stillborn infant.

"Wait here," he said.

He walked back to his horse, passing Denver along the way. From his saddlebags he took a short-handled spade he had bought in the general store in Council Bluffs. It wasn't any good for hard digging, but it would be perfect for this.

He walked back to where Grace was standing.

"There," she said, pointing. "Try there."

Fargo walked to the spot she was indicating, tested it with his foot, and found it soft enough to dig up. He got to his knees and bit into the ground with the spade.

"How far down?" he asked.

"Not far," she said. "After all, he was very small."

Fargo dug until they judged he had dug far enough, and found nothing.

"Let's try here," he said, pointing. "You've already made a twenty-mile mistake, what's a few feet more?"

"All right."

He moved, got to his knees, and starting digging again. Before long his spade hit something.

"That's it!" she said.

"Looks like . . . old burlap," he said. "The spade's going right through it."

"Take it out!" Grace said, anxiously.

Before Fargo could he heard a familiar sound, of the hammer being cocked on a gun. He looked up and saw Billy Denver pointing his gun at him.

"You heard the lady," Denver said. "Take it out of there. Let's see what you've got."

"Changed your mind, Bill?" Fargo asked.

Denver shrugged.

"I'm not being paid, but maybe what's in that hole will compensate me—that and whatever money this little lady is carrying."

"You bastard!" she spat.

"You may be right about that, ma'am," Denver said. "Come on, Fargo. Haul it on out, or I'll kill you and do it myself."

Fargo bent to the task, and pried out whatever was

covered in the old burlap. He got both hands underneath it and pulled it out without having it fall apart on him.

"Stay on your knees, Fargo," Denver said. "Just drop the bundle."

He did as he was told. He tossed the bundle so that it landed on the ground with a thud, and the old burlap burst open to reveal its contents.

"What the hell—" Denver said. "Bones?"

"Very small bones," Fargo said. Apparently, Grace had been telling the truth all along. She'd buried her infant son out here.

"There's got to be something else in that hole," Denver said. He stepped forward and nudged the bones with his boot. "Why else would those three—I mean, why would she—"

"Stop it," she said. "Don't do that!"

She charged Denver but he easily pushed her away.

"Dig some more!"

Fargo picked up the small spade, dug into the soft earth in the hole, and tossed it up into Billy Denver's face. Denver pulled the trigger, but Fargo was already moving out of the way, rolling and coming up with his own gun in hand, firing one shot. The bullet hit Denver square in the middle of his belly. He grunted, dropped his gun, grabbed his belly, and fell to the ground.

"You're gut shot, Billy," Fargo said. "It'll take you a while to die."

Grace bent over, picked up Denver's fallen gun, and said, "No it won't," and shot the man in the head. When she saw what she had done, she fell to her knees and vomited into the dirt.

"You son of a bitch," she hissed at the dead man, and then turned to kneel over the bones of her dead son.

"We found him, Fargo," she said. "We found him."

"Yes, Grace," Fargo said, holstering his gun, "we did."

LOOKING FORWARD!
The following is the opening section from the next
novel in the exciting *Trailsman* series from Signet:

THE TRAILSMAN #208

ARIZONA RENEGADES

1861—a baked hellhole soon to be known
as the Arizona Territory, where hatred, greed,
and blood lust cost countless lives.

Apaches had been stalking the big man in buckskins for
half an hour.

Most men would not have realized it. For a typical
townsman or settler, the day was ideal for travel. Scat-
tered clouds floated lazily in a vivid blue sky, wafted by
a warm breeze from the southwest. The same breeze
stirred the grama grass so it rippled like waves on an
ocean. Here and there yucca trees poked skyward like
small islands.

The countryside was picturesque and peaceful but the
big man on the pinto wasn't fooled by appearances. It

was too peaceful, too quiet. Birds should be singing. Rabbits and lizards, usually so plentiful, were nowhere to be seen. Except for the rustling of the grass, the only sounds were the clomp of the Ovaro's hooves and the creak of saddle leather.

Skye Fargo shifted to scan the gently rolling country on both sides of the rutted dirt road he followed. His piercing lake blue eyes narrowed when he spotted grass that bent much further than it should. His ears pricked at the scrape of a knee on earth, a sound so faint no townsman or settler would have heard it.

Fargo's senses were not like those of most men. Years of living in the wild had honed them like the razor edge of a bowie. His eyes were the eyes of a hawk, his ears those of a mountain lion, his nose that of a coyote. He saw and heard and smelled things not one man in a hundred would notice. It was part of the reason others called him the Trailsman, the reason why he was widely regarded as one of the best scouts alive. Put simply, his wilderness savvy was second to none.

Fargo pretended not to see the grass bend, pretended he had not heard the knee scrape. He didn't want those who were stalking him to know he knew they were there. Acting as innocent as a newborn babe, he pretended to yawn while stretching to give them the notion he was much more tired than he was. When he lowered his right hand to his hip, he contrived to place it next to the smooth butt of the Colt strapped around his lean waist. His broad shoulders swiveled as he scoured the road ahead for the likeliest spot for the attack. The Apaches would strike soon. He was within seven or eight miles of the San Simon River and the stage station on its east bank.

Personally, Fargo would be glad to get there. The most dangerous part of his journey would be over. He had done as he promised, and once he crossed the Sam Simon, he could get on with his own affairs. Maybe head for San Antonio, and from there north to Denver to look up an old friend. The thought of her silken hair and lush body brought a smile to his dry lips. A smile that turned into a scowl of annoyance for letting his mind drift at the worst possible moment. He must stay alert or he would pay for his folly with his life.

Apaches rarely made mistakes. They were fierce fighters, proud and independent. Of late their attacks had grown more frequent, more savage, as they struggled to resist the white tide washing over their land.

Until five or six months ago things had been relatively quiet. Except for an occasional raid on a ranch or way station, the Apaches had been content to stay in their mountain retreats. Then all hell busted loose. Rumor had it a new leader was to blame. A young hothead who went by the name of Chipota was stirring the tribes up, saying the only way to rid their land of the hated whites was to unite. To rise up as one and drive their enemies out in the greatest bloodbath in Apache history.

Up ahead a knoll appeared. Fargo stayed in the middle of the road so he would have a split-second warning should warriors rush from either side. Not many were stalking him; the two he had pinpointed, possibly a couple more.

That the Apaches had shadowed him for so long without doing anything was somewhat surprising. Fargo had passed several likely spots for an ambush, yet they never jumped him. He reckoned they were up to one of their notorious tricks, that they had something special in mind which would guarantee success. His life depended on figuring out what that trick was.

Apaches were supremely wary by nature. They never took needless chances, never ran the risk of losing one of their own if it could be avoided. From infancy, Apache males were rigorously schooled in the Apache virtue of killing without being killed, and stealing without being caught. This creed was everything to them, the code, as it were, on which their whole lives were based.

The open ground worked in Fargo's favor. There were no boulders for Apaches to hide behind, no ravines or clefts in which to secrete themselves. The only cover was the grama grass—but that was enough where Apaches were concerned. They were masters at blending into the background, at appearing as part of any landscape. Apaches could literally hide in plain sight.

Fargo arched his back as if he had a kink in it, when really he wanted to rise a little higher so he could probe the grass bordering the knoll. The top was barren, worn by wind as well as the passage of countless horses, oxen, and mules.

The Ovaro suddenly pricked its ears and nickered. Fargo had no idea why. The road was empty, and there was nowhere on the barren knoll for Apaches to hide. He wondered if the pinto had caught the scent of a warrior lurking in the grass.

Fargo firmed his grip on the Colt but didn't draw. Doing so would let the Apaches know he was on to them. Crazy as it sounded, Fargo *wanted* them to spring their ambush. He would rather they tried to make buzzard bait of him than a family of unsuspecting pilgrims or merchants freighting goods. The average trader didn't stand a prayer. Which was why army patrols were so frequent, or had been until just recently.

At the base of the knoll the Ovaro abruptly snorted and shied. Fargo had to goad it on, his puzzlement growing since he still saw nothing to account for it. The warrior he'd heard earlier was off to the left and slightly to the rear. Another Apache was on the right, maybe forty feet out. Neither showed any inclination to venture nearer. Why, then, was the Ovaro so bothered?

Fargo started up the gentle slope. Countless wheels had worn deep ruts. Numerous hooves had hammered the earth until it was hard-packed. To the north a red hawk wheeled high in the sky. To the east, rising plumes of dust caught Fargo's eye and he swore under his breath. Riders or a wagon were approaching. The Apaches must already know. Maybe they were lying low because they wanted to take more lives than that of a lone horseman.

Troubled, Fargo reined up. He had an urge to pull his hat brim low against the harsh sun but he didn't take his hand off the Colt. Another check of the grama grass was unrewarding. Mulling over whether to hurry on and warn whoever was approaching, he idly glanced at the ground, at a patch of earth near the road's edge. Something about it spiked his interest although at first he could not say what it was. The ground looked *different*, somehow. Fargo glanced away, then gazed at it again. Yes, the soil had definitely been disturbed. It was looser, small clumps proof it had been freshly churned, possibly by Apache mounts.

However, when Fargo peered intently at the spot, no hoofprints were evident. There were none at all. Which was odd since tracks were everywhere else. It was as if the earth had been wiped clean, just like a schoolboy's slate.

Fargo noticed the size and shape of the disturbed soil, an area roughly six feet long and three feet wide. Then he noticed something else, his breath catching in his throat. Jutting from the ground, not more than a fingernail high, was what appeared to be the stump of a weed that had taken root. Only it was circular and hollow and more closely resembled a *reed* than a weed. The kind of hollow reeds found along certain streams. The kind a man could breathe through while underwater.

Fargo quietly dismounted, letting the reins dangle. He slowly advanced, aware grass to the north was bending toward him in a beeline. Squatting, he used his left hand to scoop up a handful of the fine dirt.

The grass to the north was bending faster and faster but Fargo ignored it and held his hand over the reed. Carefully, he tilted his palm so the dirt trickled into the opening.

A muffled grunt was the reaction. Tense seconds

passed, then the ground exploded upward, erupting like a volcano, spewing earth and dust and the stocky body of a near-naked warrior. The Apache had a revolver in one hand, a long knife in the other. He blinked to clear his vision.

Fargo's Colt leaped out and up. Instead of shooting the warrior, Fargo slammed the Colt's barrel across his forehead hard enough to split stone. The man crumpled like wet paper.

The patter of rushing feet whipped Fargo around. Another Apache was almost on top of him. This one had a revolver on either hip and a rifle slung across his back but he had not resorted to them. Clutched in his right hand was a fine knife with an ivory hilt and elaborate etchings similar to some Fargo had seen south of the border. It was already upraised for a fatal stab. But as swift as the warrior was, he couldn't match the flick of Fargo's thumb and finger. Fargo's Colt boomed twice in rapid succession. As if smashed by an invisible fist, the Apache was flung backward and lay in a disjointed heap.

The blasts drowned out the approach of a third man. Fargo barely heard him in time. Spinning, he had to fling an arm out as another knife descended. Steel rang on steel, the Colt deflecting the blade. The jolt of the impact sent the Colt flying from Fargo's hand. Suddenly he was unarmed, pitted against an enemy who would give no quarter, show no mercy.

Fargo backpedaled as the Apache closed in, the knife weaving a glittering tapestry, slashing high and low, back and forth, up and down. Fargo had no means to retaliate;

all he could do was continue to retreat, straight into the grass. Which seemed to be the warrior's intention. For the moment Fargo stepped off the road, the Apache grinned slyly, then bounded to one side and came at Fargo from a new direction.

Fargo twisted, and found out why the warrior had grinned. The grama grass clung to his legs, impeding him. Not much, yet just enough so he was unable to fully evade the next swing. The knife sliced through several of the whangs on his sleeve. Another inch, and it would have bit deep into his wrist.

Grunting, the Apache pressed his assault. He was shorter than Fargo but stouter and superbly muscled. Fargo crouched, making it harder for the warrior to strike a vital organ. He was ready when the blade flashed out again. So did his left hand. He seized the Apache's wrist but to his dismay he couldn't hold on. It felt as if the man's skin were covered with oil. Fargo should have remembered. Apaches often greased their bodies before going on raids, rendering them nearly impossible to grapple with at close quarters.

Fargo dipped to slide a hand into his right boot but the warrior was on him before he could grab the Arkansas toothpick secreted there.

Again the Apache flung his knife arm on high. Again Fargo brought up his arms to ward off the blow. But this time an unforeseen misstep turned the tide of battle in the warrior's favor. As Fargo brought up his arms, he tripped over a cluster of stems. He flailed to stay upright and was on the verge of straightening when the Apache lowered a shoulder and rammed into him with all the power of a bull gone amok.

Fargo crashed onto his back. Frantically, he tried to lever upward but the warrior pounced, landing on his chest. The breath whooshed from his lungs as the Apache straddled him. Glittering dark eyes regarded him with raw delight. Fargo attempted to rise but the man had him pinned.

Realizing it, the Apache grinned and spoke in a thickly guttural tone.

Fargo's knowledge of the Apache tongue was limited. He thought the man said something to the effect, "It gives me great joy to kill you, my enemy." The words were unimportant. The moment's delay it bought Fargo was. He heaved upward, bucking like a bronco, his hips rising a good foot off the ground.

It unbalanced the Apache but did not dislodge him. Clutching the ivory hilt in both brawny hands, the warrior elevated the blade once more.

Fargo was desperate. He couldn't reach his own knife, couldn't throw the man off. He was, in short, as good as dead. He knew it and the Apache knew it. Which explained why the warrior paused again, showing even white teeth, to savor his moment of triumph. Then, shoulders bunching, the man drove the knife at Fargo's throat.

At the very last instant Fargo wrenched his neck aside. He felt the blade scrape him, felt a stinging sensation. The Apache started to pull the knife back to try again. Fargo couldn't let that happen. Luck had been with him once. He couldn't rely on the same miracle twice. So, faster than the eye could follow, Fargo opened wide and clamped his teeth down on the Apache's wrist. He bit with all the strength his jaws could muster, shearing through flesh as if it were soft, boiled venison. The Apache yelped and tried to tear loose but Fargo literally clung on for dear life, grinding his teeth deeper. He tasted the animal fat that had been smeared on the man's body, tasted the salty tang of warm blood.

In great pain, the Apache placed his other hand against Fargo's brow and pushed, seeking to force Fargo to release him. But Fargo's teeth were almost grating on bone. More and more blood gushed. Suddenly the warrior shifted his weight so he could grab the knife with his left hand.

For a span of heartbeats the Apache was off balance. It was the opportunity Fargo needed. Bucking upward again, this time he succeeded in dislodging his adversary. The warrior tumbled to the right as Fargo rolled to the left.

Fargo came up with the Arkansas toothpick in his hand. The Apache had backed off a few feet and was holding the damaged wrist pressed against his midriff. The long knife was now in the warrior's other hand. Fargo glided in low, aiming a cut at the man's legs. Predictably, the Apache countered by lowering his own blade. But Fargo's cut was a feint. Reversing himself, he launched the toothpick up and in. Although the Apache's catlike reflexes enabled him to avoid being impaled, the toothpick's tapered tip gouged a bloody furrow.

They warily circled, the Apache's eyes blazing with

hatred. Fargo dared not take his own eyes off his foe, yet he worried other warriors were rushing to help and might be almost on top of him. He had to end the clash swiftly. Yet how, when he was up against someone as skilled as this brave was?

Fargo feinted again, then tried for a throat strike. It was no more effective than his first feint. In a flurry he tried all the techniques he had learned, all the thrusts and ruses and counters he had mastered, but each time the Apache thwarted him.

Both of them were breathing heavily from their exertions. The Apache's blade was longer, giving him greater reach, but he couldn't capitalize on the advantage. For Fargo's part, he was debating whether to dash to the road and reclaim the Colt. It puzzled him that the warrior hadn't resorted to a revolver. No sooner did he think it than the Apache did just that.

Fargo had no recourse. He sprang in closer, slicing the toothpick at the warrior's arm. The Apache's knife speared at his face but Fargo ducked under it. A Remington was rising toward him when the Arkansas toothpick connected at last, the slender blade transfixing the warrior's hand.

The Remington fell. For perhaps two seconds the two men looked into each other's eyes, taking silent measure. Then they both lunged to claim the pistol for their own. Fargo was a shade faster. His fingers wrapped around the butt and he was rising when the warrior bellowed like a bear and plowed into him, lifting Fargo clean off his feet. The long knife sought his ribs. Fargo grimaced while simultaneously jamming the muzzle against the Apache's torso, thumbing back the hammer, and firing.

At the retort, the warrior stiffened and released Fargo, who staggered back. Straightening, Fargo fired again as the Apache hurtled at him. The slug took the man in the chest and swung him completely around. Teetering, the warrior said something softly to himself, then raised his face to the sky, cried out, and pitched forward, dead.

Fargo backed toward the road. He was sore and bruised and bleeding. Recalling there might be more warriors, he turned, but the grama grass was undisturbed, the road empty save for the two prone forms.

It did not stay empty for long. As Fargo bent to pick up his Colt, the pounding of hooves and loud, familiar rattling fell on his ears. He had been so caught up in saving his hide, he had forgotten about the dust cloud to the east. Toward the knoll rushed a stage, the driver hauling on the reins and shouting for the team to stop.

"Whoa, there! Whoa! Whoa! Whoa!"

Fargo shoved the Remington under his belt and slid the toothpick into its ankle sheath. The dependable Ovaro had ventured several yards into the grass across the road and was patiently waiting. He crossed to it as the stage clattered to a stop shy of the two Apaches. The lead horses whinnied and shied, spooked by the scent of blood, but the driver knew his business and immediately brought them under control.

"Tarnation, mister! What in the hell just happened?" asked the shotgun guard, a short man whose cheek bulged with a wad of chewing tobacco.

"Ain't you got eyes, Larn?" demanded the driver, a grizzled cuss whose homespun clothes were baggy enough to qualify as a tent. A floppy hat adorned a craggy face framed by long hair speckled with gray. "Don't them Injuns give you a clue?"

"There's another in the grass," Fargo said, nodding.

The driver half rose to see better. "Lord Almighty! You kilt yourself three Apaches all by your lonesome! That takes some doin'. Either you're the toughest hombre this side of the Pecos, or you're the luckiest critter on two legs." A bushy brow arched as he raked Fargo from head to toe. "The name's Dawson, by the way. Buck Dawson. Best damned driver the Butterfield Overland Stage Company has."

"And not too shy to tell everyone under the sun, either," the shotgun commented dryly.

Fargo gestured. "Give me a hand and you can be on your way."

Buck Dawson wrapped the reins around the brake lever, propped his whip in the boot, then gripped the rail to the driver's box to climb down. "Are you sure you got all them varmints, mister? Apaches are sneaky devils. Might be more of 'em lyin' off in the grass, waitin' to make wolf meat of us and the passengers."

"I doubt there are any others," Fargo responded. Had there been, they would surely have hurried to help their friends.

With remarkable agility for one his age, Buck swung to the ground. "Larn, you keep us covered, you hear? Just in case. We lose any of the folks inside, Clements will have us tarred and feathered." Buck grinned at Fargo, revealing that two of his upper front teeth were gone. "That'd be Charley Clements, our boss. The meanest jasper you'd ever want to meet. Why I keep on workin' for the likes of him I'll never know."

Larn chuckled. "It could be because he's the only human being who will put up with your shenanigans."

Buck Dawson moved to the bodies. "Don't listen to him, mister. He's just sore 'cause all the ladies like me better. He's younger and handsomer, but I've got more spunk. And ladies like their menfolk to have plenty of vinegar and vim."

Faces appeared at the stage window, watching as Fargo crossed the road. A man gruffly demanded, "Why have we stopped, driver? Surely we're not at another relay station so soon?"

"Surely we're not, Mr. Tucker," Buck Dawson responded with a touch of distaste. "Soon as we clear the way, we'll be off. In the meantime, hold your tater." Scrunching up his weathered face as if he had just sucked on a lemon, he whispered to Fargo, "Uppity busybody. Put some folks in a store-boughten suit and they reckon they own the world."

Dawson stopped to grab the wrists of the Apache Fargo had knocked out. Just then the warrior's eyes snapped open and he leaped erect. Dawson screeched like a woman in labor while throwing himself backward.

The Apache made no attempt to reclaim the weapons he had dropped. Pivoting, he streaked into the grass. But as fleet as he was, he couldn't outrun buckshot.

"That one's still alive!" Larn bawled, rising and pressing the scattergun to his shoulder.

"No!" Fargo shouted. He wanted the warrior alive, wanted to turn him over to the military for questioning, but Fate dictated otherwise.

At a range of twenty feet the Apache took the full brunt of a load of buckshot squarely in the back. He was lifted off his feet and thrown like a child's doll. When he hit, he catapulted end over end until finally coming to rest on his side, his limbs askew, a jagged cavity the size of a watermelon in his chest.

At the selfsame instant, with no forewarning whatsoever, the team bolted. Larn tried to grab hold of the rail on top of the stage for support but the abrupt lurch tumbled him from his perch. With no one in the seat, the stage sped off down the road. Shocked passengers gaped in alarm.

Fargo glimpsed a lovely face topped by hair the color of fire. Rotating, he reached the stallion in three bounds, gripped the apple, and was in the saddle and reining the stallion around before the rear wheel rumbled by. But by then the team was in full stride and he had to spur the pinto to catch up.

"Stop 'em! Stop 'em!" Buck Dawson raved, flapping his arms like an agitated crow taking flight.

Fargo drew abreast of the stage door. He glimpsed the redhead again and the florid face of a bearded man, both shocked by the unsettling turn of events. He lashed the reins to increase speed. In another few seconds he would be alongside the team and could bring them to a stop. But the team, running erratically, caused the stage to swerve sharply. Fargo had to veer off the road to avoid a collision. It slowed him down, costing him precious seconds, and the stage pulled ahead.

"Stop 'em! Stop 'em!" Dawson continued to yell and flap.

Stallion and rider flew like an arrow. Fargo had spent more hours in the saddle than any ten men. He was a superb horseman and he proved it now, racing to overtake the stage, then swinging wide when it swerved toward him as it had before. He could see the woman's white fingers grasping the edge of the window, hear the bearded man swearing a string of oaths.

Another man appeared. A younger man in the type of broad-brimmed hat favored in the rough and tumble cow country of central and southern Texas. He had on a faded leather vest and a shirt as well-worn as the hat. Poking his head out, he twisted so he could reach up and latch onto the top rail.

Fargo guessed what the young cowhand was going to attempt and admired the man's grit. The passengers were being bounced around like so many thimbles in a sewing box, so it was hard for the cowhand to keep hold of the rail. He did, though, slowly pulling himself upward. One slip and he would be dashed to the ground with possibly fatal results.

"Leave it to me!" Fargo hollered.

Either the cowhand couldn't hear over the din or else he thought he could stop the stage sooner on his own because he kept pulling himself higher. He had both hands wrapped around the rail now and over half his body was outside the coach.

Fargo was a few yards behind it and to one side. He dared not ride directly in its wake and have dust spew into his face, into his eyes and nose and ears, blinding him and making him cough. A straight stretch materialized. Fargo could gain ground if he wanted, perhaps even pull up next to the team, but he hung back on a hunch the young cowhand was biting off more than he could chew.

Within seconds the hunch was borne out. Clinging to the rail, his whole body swaying violently, the young man eased his legs from the window. All that were left were his boots. But as he hauled himself higher, one of his spurs snagged on the window. He tugged to free it just as the stage gave another jarring lurch. A hand came off the rail and the cowboy swung outward. Gritting his teeth, he clung on, then propelled himself toward the top. He almost made it.

The front wheel hit a hole and the whole stage seemed to bounce in the air. The cowboy's other hand was jarred free and he dropped.

A scream tore from the redhead.

Fargo reined in perilously close to the coach and looped an arm around the man's waist. A yank, a slap of his legs, and they were clear of the rear wheel. The stage pounded on while Fargo slowed to deposit his burden.

The cowboy looked up. "Save them, mister! There are two women inside!"

Fargo needed no encouragement. He let go, then goaded the Ovaro into a gallop. In a way, the passengers were fortunate the team had spooked on the flatland and not up in the mountains where sheer cliffs often bordered the road. All Fargo needed was another minute or two and he would end their ordeal.

Then another head poked out the window on the other side of the stage. A head adorned with long blond curls. It was a woman, and she was trying to do the same as the cowboy.

Fargo rode for all he was worth.